THE RAINBOW SINGER

THE RAINBOW SINGER

A NOVEL

SIMON KERR

THEIA . AN IMPRINT OF HYPERION . NEW YORK

Library of Congress Cataloging-in-Publication Data

Kerr, Simon
    The rainbow singer : a novel / Simon Kerr.—1st ed.
    p. cm.
    ISBN 0-7868-6798-1
    1. Belfast (Northern Ireland)—Fiction. 2. Irish—United States—Fiction. 3.
Protestants—Fiction. 4. Prisoners—Fiction. 5. Wisconsin—Fiction. 6. Young
men—Fiction. I. Title.

PR6111.E77 R35 2002
823'.92—dc21   2001052288

Hyperion books are available for special promotions and premiums.
For details contact Hyperion Special Markets, 77 West 66th Street, 11th floor,
New York, New York, 10023, or call 212-456-0100.

FIRST EDITION

Designed by Debbie Glasserman

10 9 8 7 6 5 4 3 2 1

To Caroline
Who shows me what love can be.

ACKNOWLEDGMENTS

Special ta to the Duchess of Dork, who gave her Duke the time to try and fail, and eventually succeed.

Passive/aggressive tas to my Mum and Dad for raising me entirely the wrong way for me. Ta for listening as I learned to Dr. Colin Edwards, tutor at the highly successful School of Creative Writing, Bath Spa University College, England (you guys owe me big-time for this plug, OK?). Tas to Simon Trewin and Emma Parry, my favorite mercenaries in all the world. Also, ta to Leigh Haber, the chosen Mom of this precocious ferocious little book.

ONE

1 | THE RAINBOW OF HOPE

If you really want to hear about it, there's a few things you should know about Project Ulster before I really kick off on the story improper. It was promoted in the throat-cutting churches and chapels of Northern Ireland with the slogan "The Rainbow of Hope." The pot of gold at the end of this rainbow was the relative peace of the unwild Midwest USA. And I think, though I may be wrong, that they had that *Red and yellow and pink and green, orange and purple and blue, I can sing a rainbow, sing a rainbow, sing a rainbow too* as their theme song.

Not exactly Iron Maiden is it? So did I sing their rainbow—aye, I did like fuck!

...

My name, the good Prod name my parents gave me, is Wil Carson: Wil after the Father of Ulster, King Billy; Carson after being related to the savior of Partition, Lord Carson.

I was sold the Rainbow of Hope on the last Sunday in the pissing wet May of 1985. Yeah, it's been fifteen long years, first in Lincoln Hills School for Juvenile Offenders and then in the Green Bay Correctional Institution, but I can still say what May day it was. I was sold out on the twenty-seventh. My Ma was the Project salesman, or should that be saleswoman, or even the salesperson? Doesn't matter, it doesn't do to be too PC or people think you're weak.

Anyway, as I was trying to say, we were in the living room after Sunday lunch when my Ma stops her claw-fingered knitting, takes off her horn-rimmed NHS glasses, and comes right out with it: "You know, Wil, I was chatting away to Pastor Good at the end of the service and well, he says you could go to America for a month scot-free."

Now I was sitting right in front of the TV at the time, watching El Cid hay-bed Sophia Loren and fiddling mightily with my ucksters, so I didn't think I heard her right. "What's that you say, Ma?"

"The Pastor has put your name up as a substitute for Project Ulster."

"Do what?"

All of a sudden she had my full attention. I don't think my Ma was used to getting anybody's full attention ever, certainly not me or my Da's, so she became a little self-conscious. She might even have blushed some when she said, "Someone dropped out. Wouldn't you like to go on a holiday, son?"

"You're fucking dead right I would!"

I got a right slap around the gob for saying that, but any fourteen-year-old no-hoper from the back streets of East Belfast would have done the same thing and cursed his good fortune.

Looking back on it, though, I think: is that what did it for me? But then I get to thinking—What is a blessing? What is a curse? What is a fortune after all? And it beats the fuck out of me. Life has always been a mixing up of the good and the bad and the me. Things I think will be good don't turn out that way. Things I dread doing I end up enjoying. I've tried reversing things, the polarity of fate, you know like turning the positive into the negative before it occurs, but nah, that doesn't work. Maybe if I hadn't mocked my future my past wouldn't have been mapped out that way? But then how are you supposed to consider your future at the time? Or your present. Or your past for that matter? In terms of the blessings you receive or the curses? In terms of good and bad? Who the hell knows what good or bad really is? Can morality be applied to a life's chronology? The very thought is a bag of shite. We're all taught Plato's morality (wrapped up in Christianity) and I read in the prison library that Plato used to fuck young boys up the arse. I didn't make my life

happen. Time made me. Place made me. Why am I supposed to regret what I did when I was brought up by God-
loving, God-fearing Christians to do it? They taught me to
call people Taigs, and hate those they said were Taigs, so
like a good Prod I hated Taigs so much I could have killed
every last one of them.

I'll tell you something else for nothing—I hated them Taigs
a fuckload more later on that pissing Sunday. Right after the
evening service, the stiff-lipped ol' Pastor told my Ma and
me, "Now, Wil, you know what the Project is?"

"Nah," I said. "Tell us."

The Pastor cleared his throat like he always did prior to
preaching. "From what I've heard, which I'll admit isn't
much at this late stage, it's about the Americans bringing
you to America to teach you about peace and reconciliation, son."

I said, "Right?"

"They want to help us take the gun out of our politics,
son."

I said, "They do, do they?"

"Yes. They want to help us stop the youth of today
becoming involved in paramilitary groups."

I said, "Aye—you're kidding?"

But he wasn't. He looked deadly serious. I had to choke
back a laugh.

"And if you're going, Wil," the Pastor went on, "you'll
be going with nine other God-fearing Protestants your
own age."

At that point I cheered and punched the air. That sounded great!

Then he added, "And as I understand it, given the conditions of the Project, ten Catholics."

"Taigs?" I spat the word out.

"Wil!" said Ma.

"Ten Taigs!" I said again.

The ol' Pastor corrected me, "Catholics, son. Catholics."

I thumped my Bible on my thigh and walked away. "No way," I said. "No way, José!"

Ma chased me out of church. "Don't be like that, Wil!" she shouted.

I looked back in anger. It's funny, I can still see that moment. She was small, frail under the cross—the gold cross hanging over the church door. If she'd only known her own wee son was imagining her martyr carcass nailed up there. The Crucifixion of St. Ma, Jesus H. Christ, forgive us our trespasses.

"You should have told me the catch!" I yelled at her. And I stomped home the long way through our estate, by myself, in the pissing dusk. It was always pissing down on me—and that isn't just me projecting my mood onto recollections of the weather.

I mean, I was so gutted at losing out on that trip. And yet, thinking about it objectively, or as objectively as any individual can get, what did the loss of the American Dream mean to me then? A lot and not a lot of nonsense.

I would never see the Hollywood sign on that hill.

I would never be driven or drive in a pink Cadillac.

I would never gorge on burgers.

I would never see a Van Halen concert.

I would never see naked sorority girls' tits and arses and beavers like in that movie *Porky's*.

I would never be given an American Football helmet as a souvenir of my trip.

Worst of all, I would not be able to boast I'd done or got · any of these things to my schoolmates at Belvoir High when I came back.

All thanks to them ten faceless Taigs!

2 THE FREEDOM OF ULSTER

Over the last few days of May, Ma tried her best to turn my head with stories of how peace and reconciliation was a good Christian aim and how *Happy Days* was made in Milwaukee, but I wasn't listening. I'd busied myself with other stuff and, as usual, she ended up spitting these words into my face: "Why can't you just listen to me for once, you stubborn little brute?"

See, what with Ma trying to be so middle class, she didn't realize I was an up-and-coming member of the Belvoir Brigade of the Third Batallion, the Ulster Freedom Fighters: UFF for short. The reason she didn't know is that I was careful, and rightly so: she would have killed me if she'd found out, or at least kicked me out of the house. And then I would have had to go live with my Da and his Ma in the badlands of Armagh and that just wasn't on. There were too many fucking Taigs down there.

I honestly did think about going public at school, for the terrorist kudos, you know, like to fit in better but, nah. It would have found its way back to Ma on the rumor machine somehow. I took the advice of Al the alco, my CO: "Aw fuck, you don't want to come out, son. There's too many Taigs out there. Even one knowing who you are and what you do is too many. Keep the balaclava on and the head down."

The Belvoir Brigade used to seriously terrorize the Taigs near our estate. I say near, because no Taig in his or her right mind would live on it. I mean, we were what I reckon is the first Heavy Metal song—Eddie Cochran's "Something Else"—when it came to intimidation and there wasn't one of us over eighteen.

The week I rejected Project Ulster we were tasked with clearing a place name of Kimberly Close of three unwanted Taig families. You see, Taigs in your street lowered the property values, so it was their own neighbors that wanted shot of them. The Kimberly Close Prods paid the UFF protection money to do the job because they didn't want to get their hands dirty. We were to be their hands, the Hit Squad. We didn't mind getting our hands dirty, or bloody for that matter. Only problem was, there was four of us, and there must have been forty of them Taigs, women and kids included.

On the Monday me, Wee Sammy, Brian and squad leader Rick the Prick started with the family on the corner and, tins hissing like snakes, sprayed their house with all sorts of red, white and blue acronyms during the first night: things like FTP (Fuck The Pope) + IRA, UFF, and what have you. Sure enough, they got the message and packed up the next day.

The other two families though were made of sterner stuff. We tried the territory marking shite on Tuesday: no deal. We bricked their front windows Wednesday, when *Coronation Street* was on. Thursday, we mitched off school and burned their cars in broad daylight: no dice. That forced Al the alco into it. He met us at our regular RV, in other words behind the school bikesheds, and tache and tats shaking in a fit of the pre-liquid-lunch DTs, he ordered the petrol bombings at four o'clock that morning. You see four A.M. is when most people die of natural causes. They say it's down to circadian rhythms. The human body isn't on the ball at that time, it wants to be asleep. So four's when SAS Troopers choose to attack enemy sentries. It's the real witching hour, when people can die of unnatural causes too.

I snuck out at three and joined the boys by the woods, dark and deep (Ma was a heavy snorer). We flitted down Finaghy Road keeping to the shadows. When we got to Kimberly Close we simultaneously lobbed two Molotov

cocktails into each Taig house. Our targets—the upstairs
bedroom windows. Why the upstairs?—because the Taigs'd
have to get downstairs and out the front door sharpish.
House clearance. Minimal damage. Mission accomplished
and all by the beginning of June.

I regret to say two young girls were burned but everyone
got out alive.

Ethnic cleansing. That's the term for what we did all right,
and we have it in our everyday language thanks to those
other good Prods, the Serbs. I wonder how many Serbian
boys thought they were doing the right thing in Bosnia? I
know I was fooled into believing what I was told way back
then, but this is now. And I told you—even though I didn't
have to—because I want you to know that I've done some
things of . . . well, dubious virtue, in the name of the
Father. I had dirty hands even at fourteen.

I'm not a guilty man because I wasn't a guilty boy, but
like I say, I have my regrets.

Yeah I do.

And I know what I'm about to ask you is hard, but try
not to judge; try to understand. I was young. Older men,
all father figures, exploited my youthful innocence and exu-
berance. In a patriarchal society the son must act in a way
that pleases the Father or the Big Brother or the animus or
whatever you want to call it. There is no other choice but
loyalty.

. . .

My Da was the patriarchal animus of Ulster if ever it was personified. Woe betide me if I went against his will. He was furious fast with his fists. That was why Ma'd left him and took me with her. They were separated now and heading for divorce but she wasn't averse to using him to coerce me into doing things. And Ma wanted me to go on the Project so she phoned Da—

What do you know, the first Saturday in June there was Da on our doorstep looking singularly pissed off—as usual.

Ma let him in without the regular slanging match. That was a bad sign. It meant he had come especially to give me a talking to.

Now Da was a big bigot. Six foot one was the height he claimed he was but he was more likely less than six foot: his side of the family always had to exaggerate and elaborate on the truth (except me that is). It wasn't my Da's height that made people say he was big. It was more because of his big-boned, sinewy width and girth. And then there was his beer belly—it hung there like he was pregnant, like he could give birth to another son, a better one, at any minute.

We went into the living room, him and me.

Ma took to making the tea.

"Bout ye, son," said Da. He sat down on the couch.

"Hanging together, Da," I replied and kerplunked down on the floor in front of him.

"I hear you've been offered a chance to go to the U.S., son." Da was always straight to the point, no messing.

"Aye. But I'm not going."

Da stared hard at me. He had dead eyes, hard dead blue eyes that'd lost all hope, all life of their own. "Why'd that be?" he said.

"The Taigs. They're taking Taigs with Prods. It's some jiggery-popery or other."

Da seemed to take an age to consider this protest. It had merit to the big bigot in him, no doubt. But he had a job to do, and he would do it for peace of mind or Ma would deny him that forever. "Your Ma says you'd be staying with a Prod family. A Presbyterian Reverend no less." Da sounded suitably reverential. See, he professed to being religiously religious but it seemed to me his belief system was based solely on the all-day Sunday worship of Guinness. He didn't go to church but claimed he didn't need to; his father had brought him up the right way, you know?

"Da, I'm no Presbyterian," I said after a bit.

"Listen, son. Never look a gift horse in the mouth. So what if it's got a few rotten teeth. It's free and you can pull them out later. Get it?"

"I think so, Da." I got the gist, though my interpretation of the analogy was a little more extreme than his. Gift horse—pulling teeth—beating up on Taigs—you know? Yeah, that horse he gifted me would become a twisted symbol for both my Freudian destrudo and libido all right. At the end of the Project it twisted into an iron horse called Suzi. And then it warped into a deer of all things?

Da said, "Good, so I'll bung your Ma some pocket money for you and you'll go."

Woe betide me.

I lied earlier when I was talking about loyalty, or rather didn't tell the whole truth in that context. Sorry, it's all too easy to do. There is another choice to loyalty. Excommunication. Group death. The removal of approval, and with it the protection of others. But that is not something a fourteen-year-old could rightly be expected to choose, is it?

3 ROCKING THE GIFT HORSE

I found myself going to my first meeting of the Projectees the next Saturday. The ol' Pastor was late collecting me, and he drove me to this barbecue wingding down at Crawfordsburn Beach like Meatloaf's *Bat Out of Hell*.

He quickly handed me over to the Prod counsellor who went by the name of Kate. She was small and round, and with a small voice, called together all those hangers-on who weren't eating, paddling or playing football. Like Ma would have done, she introduced me as the new boy: "Everybody say hello to Wil."

I went red like I always did when I was meeting new people, then all-over crimson; the color was a deep mix of impotent rage and embarrassment at her mollycoddling.

The Taig counsellor, Ciaran, a tall scarecrow of a man, was the first to shake my reluctant red hand of Ulster. Now, I had never knowingly touched a Taig before, let alone shaken the hand of one. Contamination. I wiped my hand on my jeans right after so he saw it. And I saw the anger flare in his eyes, along with something I now know was pity because I too pity my young self.

I stood there for a moment on my own. Then this huge man-boy came up to me. "I'm Michael," he boomed with a well-broken voice. I looked up at him. He had a Prod face—no telltale cyclops eye (at the time I was made to believe in eugenic mythology). The sun made a halo around his big bourgeois head. Michael was six foot three at the age of fifteen. A fully mature male. He made me feel small and weedy (I'm six two now, but at that age I think I was about five six). I didn't much like Michael but I didn't much hate him either. He was just the kind of Prod I could never be; life had blessed him with too many gifts; he didn't have to fight for his place in any of it.

Of the succession of other milling Prods and Taigs that bothered to introduce themselves to me, girls and fellas, nobody made much of an impression. Except for the obvious Taigs, who obviously made me sick. Then, way down the pecking order I met Phil. He was a Prod too. A small Prod too. I liked that about him instantly. I also liked the Iron Maiden T-shirt he was wearing—*The Trooper*. That, and his long black mop confirmed him as a Metaller. He must have seen I was wearing a Van Halen *5150* T-shirt and that I had long black mop and that I was a Metaller too. He grinned that infectious mischievous grin of his as we shook hands: Wil and Phil. I knew I had a friend for this trip—if not for life.

Phil and me talked about the recent Van Halen split. We agreed how unfair it was that Dave Lee Roth had been kicked out of Van Halen but that Sammy Hagar sounded all right on the new album.

After having a hot dog or two we got into a football match with some Taigs. It was in this contest, with me playing within the rules of the Bootiful Game, that I was fouled. Yeah, dirty hacking brutality entered my life on the end of a Taig's leg. And I discovered my first personal Taig enemies. See up till that shin-rattling hack, my hate for Taigs was as if they all wore Gerry Adams masks: it was inbred, impersonal, idealistic.

I want you to remember it was them two who started it.

I name Peter Byrne the hacker.

I name Seamus Finnegan as his backer.

I got up from the foul—which occured right in front of goal and would have been a penalty if there had been a referee, and I went for the hacker.

I'd got Peter by the neck of his Gaelic shirt and was shouting into his cheeky wee leprechaun mug "You cheating halion!" when Seamus weighed in.

Peter wasn't small but I wasn't scared of him. Seamus was a different matter. He was a tall and rangy build, and as Da would have said, he'd an evil eye set in his cyclops face. (That was one of Da's staple sayings to legitimize why he wouldn't trust Taigs. All part of my rich psycho-socio-politico-historico-economic inheritance. You can't blame me for repeating his mistakes. Nobody can.)

I can still see psycho-clops Seamus raring for a fight. With his evil eye glowing green, he might even have been some IRA assassin . . . All right, forget it, that's just me echoing my bigoted father. Truth is, before I knew it, I found myself dragged off Peter and wrestled to the ground.

I heard Phil say, "Fairplay, Seamus. Leave him be."

But Phil was no match for Peter, let alone Seamus, and Seamus was too busy playing the big man, shoving my head into the sand. Seamus raised his fist over my face. "Give up?"

"Nah!" I hissed.

Peter kicked me in the ribs. "Give up, Proddy!" he said.

I wouldn't. I kicked and screamed and fought but I couldn't get Seamus off me.

I could see Big Michael and some of the other Prods getting edgy. One of their own was down.

It took the intervention of Counsellor Ciaran to stop the scrap spreading along sectarian lines. He dragged us apart with: "That's enough, lads. Enough!" He told the rest: "There'll be no more football today."

Right enough there was no more football that day, thanks to the pitiful anger of Counsellor Ciaran. I say thanks to him because I would only have turned it into murderball and that would have been a waste. Anyone who watched

The Godfather as many times as I had knew that revenge was
a dish best served cold.

I look upon that skirmish as Round One. No blood was spilt
but I lost. I lost. But, then again, if I hadn't have lost I wouldn't
have met Teresa. When Phil was helping me dust the sand off
myself she came over to me. "I'm sorry," she said. That disarmed me. I could tell she was a Taig but I thought it was
decent of her to apologize on behalf of her kith and kind for the
assault. And her face disarmed me more. She wasn't beautiful
like your woman Sophia Loren but in a Taigy, bewitchy kind
of way I had not seen before (I now know the word is eldritch).

"It's not your fault," I said.

She swept long strands of blue-black hair away from her
face. "No, but he's a friend of mine."

"Unlucky you," I replied.

"I'm Teresa," she said.

"Wil," I said curtly. "Wil Carson."

"Nice meeting you, Wil," she said, and somehow with
this strange intense look, she left me aware that I was completely alone in the world.

You know they say the eyes are the windows of the
soul?—Well, this is going to sound soppy, but I'll swear
there was something in those windows of hers I needed to
stop that feeling of loneliness.

Even though she was a Taig.

Even though she was my enemy.

Even though we have no souls.

There were a couple of other meetings in June but they were low-key affairs, dress rehearsals for this concert the Americans wanted us Projectees to throw for them. Nothing much happened, like I say. I avoided Seamus and Peter, and Teresa, and hung around with Phil. We talked a lot. But never about our lives. Our discussions were about whether or not Rainbow's singer, Ronnie James Dio, actually was the devil, or whether Ozzy did eat bats live on stage, or whether Alice Cooper was the keeper of the Serpent from the Garden of Eden. Yeah, hanging with Phil was a good laugh.

One thing that sticks out in my mind is—we were coached how to sing (in my case mime) "When Irish Eyes Are Smiling" by an ol' doll piano teacher the name of Heidi Burren.

The shame of even being in the same room when Taig songs were being sung! When Irish eyes are smiling, indeed. The only time Irish eyes are smiling is when one of us Brits gets it in the neck. At least that's what Loyalist history—the word-of-mouth version of it—would have you believe. And culture is hard to forget.

Something else, on a lighter note, that's hard to forget too, was the incident with the theme song. That killed me. We were all singing or miming on stage, Taigs and Prods, in this old rickety church hall they'd rented for practice. When we got to the *I can sing a rainbow, sing a rainbow, sing a*

rainbow too bit Phil started to growl the words like your
man James Hetfield out of Metallica. I creased up and
couldn't stop laughing. That kicked the hyena in Phil off.

Ol' doll Burren lost the rag with us two. She was ranting
and raving at us to stop. But we couldn't. She just killed us
more. And then other people on stage started to laugh without knowing really why. You know the way it happens.
Pretty soon most everybody was dominoed into laughing.
And she thought it was at her. She stormed out swearing to
God she'd never be back to a red-faced Ciaran and Kate.
That was even funnier. I must have laughed for a full five
minutes flat. My ribs were sore for two days after.

Funny, all that makes me smile even now. I have to admit
it, I was enjoying the Prod bit of the Project.

Same way I never told Project Ulster about the UFF, I never told any of the Hit Squad I was going to America or what I was doing with myself when I was at those dopey rehearsals. They asked all right, especially that noseybonk, Rick the Prick. I just told him I was seeing more of my Da. I had to lie. No self-respecting Loyalist could rise through the ranks after admitting he'd fraternized with the enemy, let alone holidayed with them.

So you see, going to America for a month posed a big big problem for me. I'd had to lie to the squad and then I had to lie really convincingly to Al to get some leave. I met him in his club after my tea, the Friday before the flight. He was trolleyed when I told him my cover story: "I'm been sent away to my Aunty Fay's in England for a month starting tomorrow, Al."

"The first of July?" he blew up. "Aw for fuck's sake!"

Now Al was a mean drunk so I kept my mouth shut and my distance from him—in case he twatted me one.

"You know July is our busiest month!" he ranted on. "Why didn't you tell me sooner, son?"

"Ma sprang it on me. She doesn't want me making trouble around the Twelfth."

"Yer Ma! The womenfolk never get it, do they? There's a fucking war on and she's sending you off to your Aunty's." He shook his head violently and slurred, "Aw fuck me, you better do what your Ma says."

They say travel broadens the mind don't they, but I found that on the journey to America mine narrowed further. A ten-hour coach trip from Belfast, through Saturday and into the night, to Shannon Airport in the Irish Banana Republic, will start the narrowing process in a person at the best of times. At the worst of times when you have to watch your enemies move in on the girl you like—even though you don't want to—the mind turns in on itself, on the comforting restrictions of what it knows like a bear trap. Did you know that America nearly opted for the bear as its national symbol instead of the bald eagle? Nah, neither did I back then. What I did know was that Ireland had opted for the AK-47 for their national symbol. Like Al always said—Eire was the only terrorist state in Europe. It was like Libya except people liked the Irish for some reason; Christ, they even invited them to join the EEC even though the Dàil still laid unlawful claim to Ulster in Articles Two and Three. I believed what Al said. I believed in the UFF. I believed in God and in Ulster, my homeland. So as we drove down through the green green miles of beautiful scenery, I never once relaxed, never once allowed myself to admire the whole island of my birth. And could you blame me?—there was I a freedom fighter in enemy territory.

Outnumbered.

Outgunned.

And, in spite of the fact that Teresa was a fucking Taig— out of my head with that big green lizard-monster of teen jealousy.

The midnight plane we boarded at Shannon International Airport was an Aer (Phil interjected Cunni-) Lingus Boeing 747: a jumbo jet. It was the like of nothing I'd ever seen before. The sheer size. All of a sudden it made the world seem really big or something, and made me feel insignificant. Maybe it was down to the 1:1 scale. You know like in Ulster we think we're yon big in our own small world? Ma always said to people she hadn't seen in years, "It's a small world." True, Ulster is a small world, but it's a small part of a much bigger whole—the world. Planet Earth. Mother Earth. It's easy to forget the size of life when you live there. Better to fool yourself with a 10:1 scale. Like you matter.

The jumbo showed me I didn't matter. It swallowed me down like the whale in the Bible, gobbling up Jonah in one gulp.

The early part of the ten-hour journey in the belly of this aluminium sky whale was a smooth one. Some Projectees freaked out or boked up but not me. I wasn't scared of flying, see. I'd been on a plane to the Costa Del Hol for a fortnight, back when I was eleven and Ma and Da were still trying hard to be man and wife.

Phil and me were sat together in a row of six empty green seats at the middle of the plane. Even before takeoff we got used to the space. We made it our own with our hand baggage. But someone from the other side saw it and came to invade. Wanted the green green fabric that was ours.

It was Teresa, with her Fenian friend Sorcha along for the ride. Now Sorcha was what you'd call a mere slip of a gingerbap. There was nothing remotely womanly about her bum, her hips or her bee-stings but she was convinced Phil would appreciate them estrogen-negative assets like crazy. Little did she know!

Teresa said, "Hi, Wil."

I grunted, "Aye."

Sorcha said, "How are you, Phil?"

Phil sighed, "Fine."

The invasion force sat down. Only not beside each other and beside us, half and half like. That would have been too polite. Sorcha sat beside Phil, to the right. Teresa rubbed past Phil and my knees and sat down on my left. We were surrounded by enemy forces. The escape routes to the aisles had been blocked off.

"Ready for the film?" Teresa asked me.

"Aye, got my headphones and all," I answered.

"Pretty crap aren't they?" she was quick to say.

"They are that," I agreed.

Teresa certainly wasn't backward at coming forward. "Do you want me to get us some blankets?" she asked.

"Blankets?" I said. I can rightly remember thinking at the time: is she trying to make me her Taigy Blanket Man, like those IRA men in the H-Blocks, but nah she wasn't, at least not intentionally.

Teresa explained, "My Dad says on long hauls the stewardesses give out blankets and a pillow for when you want to get some sleep."

"Aye, all right."

Teresa stood up and bonged the stewardess.

"Yeah, we're all going to sleep together," declared Sorcha and cuddled up to Phil.

I looked at Phil.

Phil looked at me.

I was thinking of one thing.

By the look on his face, that infectious mischievous smile of his, I thought he was after that self-same thing but, wouldn't you know, he wanted another. And it wasn't the stewardess.

...

Don't ask me because I don't know what the bloody film was we watched midway across the Pond. I could try the ol' writer's trick of reinventing the past and saying it was *The Terminator* because that fits the theme of this my own life story. But no, I'll resist that temptation. There's something tells me it was some kind of courtroom drama. That could point to *Jagged Edge* with that fella who was the government spy in *E.T.* but never quite made the Hollywood "A" list, what's-his-name . . . yeah, my nickname-sake, Peter Coyote. Or maybe I've just seen the inside of too many courtrooms in my day. Who knows?

The events in this film weren't important to the story anyway, neither were the stars. But the watching of it—that was a different matter. What happened while we all sat in front of it, in what I've read Hollywood screenwriters call the audience's negative space, and also in our positive space, that's what's of concern.

See, Phil could only take so much of Sorcha's pawing and clawing before he cracked. He lasted an hour, up to and aroundabouts where the supreme ordeal is supposed to occur in any film. You can't blame Phil. He was a polite guy, but there's only so much androgyny a fella can take, especially if it, let's say, highlights the common ground between the genders. Phil left for the longest toilet break in mile-high cinema-going history. Twenty-five minutes passed before she got the message and left Teresa alone with me.

When she'd gone Teresa started kidding around with me. I ignored her, which of course made her want to kid around

with me more. It ended up in a tickling fight which she lost
because she wanted to lose and I for some strange reason
wanted to win.

I looked down on her—yeah OK, I'd got on top and
pinned her down. Our faces were very close. I felt this terrific urge to kiss her on the lips but I didn't get a chance.

The return of Phil interrupted us. "Oi! Cut that out."

The strange reason—perhaps reason isn't the right word—I
wanted to win the wrestling, I now put it down to the fact
that love is violence. What do I mean? Is it so hard to
believe? Surely he's talking about hate, you say? Nah. Think
about it. Think about it from your own point of view. Call
up the free spirit in you, the kid or the id or the alter ego,
ask it what it thinks of love. It will speak of the unspeakable
in terms, not of endearment but ohdearment. It will say, Do
not betray your self, this can only lead from your old family
to a wife and a new family and you know what that means.
It means you will become the Tyrant Holdfast, will violently love your children and condemn them to become
emotional terrorists, fighting for their own freedom, only to
become the all-new age-old Tyrant Holdfast. Love makes
the world go around in this vicious elipse, it will say. And
yet . . .

Later in the flight, after she fell asleep, head nuzzled into
my shoulder, when I felt her eyes weep in REM and her
drool seeping into my best jumper; and much later, when I
felt her unconscious hand on the inside of my thigh, I got

this charge running through my hair, like static electricity. Or maybe it's fair to say the sensation was in my scalp. She made my hackles rise, but in a nice way, a way I'd only experienced around really boring people before: you know the kind of kid who is fascinating because they're just so, I mean how can they be so duh fatuous?

In the early hours of Sunday morning the jumbo circled Washington, D.C., in a holding pattern.

"The White House," shouted Phil. "Come and look, Wil—the White House."

I wanted to, but I was pinned by Teresa. I couldn't move without waking her. I looked helplessly at Phil.

Phil came over to my rescue. "Oi Teresa!" said Phil, shaking her. "We're here."

Teresa couldn't help but come to. She found herself in a position of some intimacy—what with her head on my shoulder and her hand in my lap. Her hand instantly flitted to loftier climbs—to get her head together. When she lifted her head though, she saw she'd drooled crusties onto me. And when she rubbed her eyes in mortified disbelief a ton of yellow sleep fell into my lap. And when she looked at the avalanche in my lap she saw my jeans tented like the Big Top. The vanity of the female of the species made her look at the circus tent a minute longer and then the other side of this self-same vanity took hold. I was going to explain that boys get pissy hard-ons in the morning but before I could, she let out a noise similar to a gargle and fled to the sanctuary of the toilet.

So callously deserted the morning after, there was nothing for it but to wipe her juices off me, think away my hardon and go for a gander at the capital city of the empire that ruled the known world. Wiping the juices away proved difficult so I took off my jumper. Thinking the hard-on away proved impossible. It needed draining physically—I shoved the shaft down and kept it below the angle required for a good prod and my circulatory system did the rest . . . Gone. Or so I thought.

I got up and joined Phil at the window. He was in front; I was behind, trying to see past his black mop.

"See that," he said. "That's Cleopatra's Needle."

Sure enough I saw that big pointy obelisk sticking up out of green green grass of America.

I was taken aback. By the sight. But also by something else—

Now, I don't know how Phil's other hand rubbed past my drained dick but it happened all right. He pretended not to notice. Out of politeness so did I. But I did seriously notice. How could I not notice? The pressure and heat started off the normal chain reaction but the speed of the rehardening took me by surprise.

Cleopatra's Needle eat your fucking heart out!

I waddled back to my seat as quickly as I could but not before Seamus, standing like my arch-nemesis in the aisle, had seen my predicament. I heard him laugh, then shout, "Carson's got a hard-on. Carson's got a hard-on!"

The chant was taken up by Peter and their other Taig cronies.

Seamus sang a solo harmony on top though. "Wil fancies Phil. Wil fancies Phil."

I should have stood up to him but there was no way I could. I felt and feel such a coward about it. It's hard to forgive myself for sitting there even now. I've tried reinventing that moment a hundred bloody times but no, I can't change it. The knowledge that bravery is as subject to timing—circadian rhythms again—as anything else doesn't really help. I had lost Round Two as well.

If only the Taig chanters and teasers had known what that event meant to me they might have stopped? I doubt it. But maybe if they'd known what it would mean to them, what I would do to repay them, they would have carried it further, made me their Jonah, bound me up and thrown me out of the Cunni-Lingus into the blue sky, to die impaled on Cleo's Needle?

Phil came and sat by me. He endured the abuse too until landing, when it died down.

"Sorry," he said when the jumbo had come to a full stop. Or at least I think he did—I may have just seen the apology in his eyes.

I took it that what he'd done had been an honest mistake.

"You're all right, Phil," I said. And I did say that out loud. He took that the wrong way though—as if I was saying I liked him too, when what I meant was, he was the only one I would exempt from revenge. Apart from Teresa—who was still in the toilet. And Big Michael, and the majority of the Prods who hadn't dishonored themselves by joining in the taunts.

In terms of earthly time, the wait in Washington, D.C., was a short one, and the flight to Milwaukee was a short one too. All told, they added another three hours onto the travel clock. However, in terms of unearthly embarrassment, I'll swear that was the longest journey in human history. There was nowhere to go to get away from Seamus and Peter. They and their mocking voices were everywhere, looming larger than life.

Phil tried to cheer me up by ripping the pish out of some new Metal Christian band called Stryper, but even a laugh or two at those buck-eejits didn't relieve the killing tension. I say "killing" because my traveling mind had narrowed to a sharp point. I knew even then, deep deep down that I was going to wreck the Project and kill me some fucking Taigs.

TWO

5 OF MURPHY AND FREDDY

You can't imagine how much I was still fuming when we arrived in Milwaukee on Sunday afternoon; it's impossible, so don't even try. The atmosphere in what the Algonquin Indians had named their Happy Hunting Ground was hot and humid, oppressive even with air-con, and I mean, I was literally shaking with adrenaline. And wouldn't you know, when we reclaimed our baggage, one of my bags was missing: the one stuffed with my best Metal T-shirts. Of course, I was the only one this happened to!

Back then, as a good little Baptist, I believed in God's will and destiny and fate and I was genuinely worried I was being punished for daring to even entertain such murderous

thoughts. But, I needn't have worried. These things are
social constructs designed to keep people denying that they
have the power to change their lives and the world of their
experience.

"Murphy's at his work all right," Phil said as we waited at
the Cunni-Lingus lost property office.

"Aye," I said. For those of you who don't know who Murphy is, think Murphy's anything that can possibly go wrong
will go wrong law; think Winnebago Indian Trickster with a
bunch of four-leafed shamrocks stuck up his arse and that
ought to put you in the picture. Would I hang this picture
on my cell wall? Yeah. Why?—because the pagan Trickster is
real, phenomenologically speaking, in the same way as the
Christian Devil is. What separates one from the other is all a
matter of degree in the mind—the group mind that is—the
most dangerous entity any individual can face. But, this isn't
the place to go into all that. That'll come later.

For now, let's just say I had to leave the airport sharpish
with the rest of the Projectees so I couldn't hang around
for my clothes. As it turns out, my Van Halen collection of
T-shirts was never found; they could still be flying around
the world to this day while their previous wearer is stuck in
here. I wish I was back in those clothes. Although, to do that
is to wish I'd never left Ulster, never seen the Void, never
found my self . . .

Cancel that wish.

We were picked up at the airport by a big yellow school
bus—the kind you see in all the movies. One in particular

flashes to mind: *Nightmare on Elm Street 2*, or was it *3*? It's the one where Freddy's wreaking dream havoc on the bus and all the earth falls away around it and it's left rocking on this solitary stack, with the kids screaming, looking down into the hell-Void.

I saw Teresa sit with Seamus and Peter. They must have told her about me for she wouldn't even look over at me. So, what else was there to do?—I stared out the windows and waited for the ground to fall away. I tried my level best to dream up Freddy the demon child-molester.

We were a sweaty hour into our journey across Milwaukee when Phil asked me, "What do you think your lot, the Horrowitz-z-zs will be like?"

"A riot," I replied.

"The Da's a minister you say?"

"Aye. A Presbyterian."

"And you're a Baptist?"

"That's right."

"What's the big difference?"

"Adult baptism."

"Oh," Phil said. He hadn't a clue what that meant. He was Church of Ireland, Anglican, if you only speak American. They didn't much believe in anything.

We sat in silence for a while then Phil said, "I reckon my lot will be a right laugh what with a name like the Kuntz-z-zs."

That killed us. Kuntz was such a stupid name. Imagine having to go through life called Kuntz. Jesus H. Christ. I don't know how long we laughed for but I can tell you it was a long time.

There was a more serious side to the whole subject of our host families though. Every Projectee except me—the substitute—was going to stay for a month with an American family of the same religious indoctrination. Each one of these families had a child of the same sex and age as us lot, except me—I was to stay with a fifteen-year-old.

Yeah, I was the odd one out all round. The odd one out of the original twenty Projectees and, if you can do simple maths in your head, with the number of Projectees double-doubling, toil and troubling when everybody meets up, I was to be the odd one out of forty. I have to say being odd is not nice at fourteen.

Unfortunately for me, the yellow school bus did not drive us to hell, it took everyone of us to the meeting point—a church hall. There, we were lined up in front of a mob of yabbering Americans and the chockablock adoption pro-ceedings took place. When they got around to calling my name out I left Phil with a high five and went to meet my host family.

6 | THE RACKET OF PROTECTION

The anti-psychiatry psychiatrist R. D. Laing says the family is the biggest protection racket in the world. And he's dead right. Pay your dues and there'll be no love trouble. Obey, and OK you won't be disciplined by our emotional or physical violence. We're bigger than you. It's run on the same rules as the rackets the Brigade had going back home.

What?—can it be that I'm saying every family's racket is the same? Nah, that's not it. The dues are the same, but the discipline, that's the variable part. Like with my Da. He didn't have to hit me. And when he hit me he didn't have to use his fists and his feet. These were choices he made—or in truth, which his Da made about him—and so on and so on back to *Planet of the Apes.* What I'm saying is that every family all around the world is not the same violent patriarchy, some are matriarchies, others may run on a liberal power-sharing basis, but each will exercise its own form of discipline on the children. They are therefore not the same, but they have to be similar for the racket to work and keep working.

I met the second-in-command racketeer of the Horrowitz-z-zs first. Ma, or should I say Mom, Horrowitz was so tiny even I almost had to pull a microscope out to see what had hugged me around the waist. Her mouth was the biggest part of her whole anatomy and, like most Americans, it shone perfect white when she smiled up at me.

"Hi, Wil," she said.

"Hi," I said.

"I'm gonna be your mom for the month," she said.

I couldn't think of anything else to say but, "Thanks for having me and all."

"Here," she said and let my waist go. "Meet my son, Derry."

"What?" I said, horrified. See Derry is not a good Prod word. It's a Taig word on account of it being the shortened version of Londonderry—see, omitting the "London" denies British sovereignty over Ulster.

"Derry," she said again.

I didn't want to look at him on principle but I had to. There was Derry stood behind her, looking like a young version of The Incredible Hulk. But don't get me wrong.

Derry wasn't green—except for his eyes. He wasn't a muscle sculpture either—although he was a big fella. And he didn't roar at me until way later on.

"Hi," I said, refusing to use his Taigy name.

"Hi," he said, looking down on me. I don't blame him. I—the substitute for a fifteen-year-old fellow Presbyterian— was so much younger and smaller than him.

We shook hands.

I took a firm grip.

His was looser.

I didn't have any good-byes to say to the Projectees that hadn't already been said, so they took me and my depleted supply of luggage to their beat-up station-wagon and drove me to my home away from home as Mom Horrowitz herself described it. She probably figured I'd be homesick. Was I homesick?—aye I was like fuck. I think deep down my small self was sick sore and tired of home even then.

Mom Horrowitz sat me up front with her on that one big front seat American cars have. I watched with some consternation as she drove off slowly and waywardly along the wrong side of the road. Then I realized that that was the right side of the road in America.

Mom Horrowitz and me made the right noises as we by-passed swathes of Milwaukee on the freeway. Polite conversation, you know. I was moaning about the trip, my lost luggage. She was saying that was terrible and that I could wear some of Derry's hand-me-downs. It was the sort of blarney ol' dolls love. I hated it, but I could do it. If I was

Irish they'd say I'd been born kissing the Blarney Stone all right—or something as twee as that. Obviously Derry hadn't even heard of Blarney Castle; he stayed quiet in the back.

"Gee, Wil, your accent is really neat," Mom Horrowitz told me and we entered into extended politeness.

I replied, and I like the way there's a hidden "lie" in the word replied, "Yours is neat too." Their accent was not neat at all. Nah. It was twangy-slangy, all long drawn-out and nasal.

After forty or so minutes, we passed by this big metal thing that looked like a UFO—just about the time the extended politeness was running out.

"What's that?" I said, genuinely interested, wondering if aliens had landed.

"It's a watertower," said Derry, like he thought I was some stupid hick from the sticks.

"Oh. What's that name on it—New Berlin?"

"Our suburb of Milwaukee," Mom Horrowitz said.

How was I to know Milwaukee had been settled largely by German immigrants, hence New Berlin and Zorro 'z's after every surname. The irony of Derry looking down on me for not knowing the local history still strikes a discord nowadays. I mean, how many Americans know anything more than their local region even. Try asking one about world history or geography or politics and see what they say. Uh. Gee whiz. Where's that? Derry probably didn't have a clue about where Ulster was, what the Troubles were, or anything.

"This is the family manse," said Mom Horrowitz as we drove up past a big wooden church to a big wooden house.

"Are all your houses made of wood?" I said.

"Mostly," said Derry.

"What about fires?"

"Huh?"

"You know, like—wood burns?"

"We have firemen here to put out fires," Mom Horrowitz said. I don't think she intended to be patronizing, but she was after all my patron so I had to let her get away with it.

We all got out of the car and I lugged my bags up to the house.

As Mom Horrowitz fumbled with the meshed outer door, I said, "Is that the Rev's church?"

"One of them," Derry said and tutted.

"How many's he got?" I said.

"Two," Mom Horrowitz said, all proud of her husband.

In Ulster, at least in the Baptist faith, they make do with one Pastor per church but there you have it, the Americans always have to go one bigger, one better.

I met Tamara—I rechristened her "Tiara"—Horrowitz, the one and only daughter, when we got inside the wooden house. She was seventeen, and a right madam to boot; still jammed at that stage where she'd realized she was so like her mom she had to do everything different just to feel like a person.

"This is Wil," said Mom Horrowitz.

"Hi," she said.

I don't think she even noticed I didn't say "Hi" back.

"Can I have the car, Mom?" Tiara said. "I was supposed to be at the mall ten minutes ago."

"What about church?" Mom Horrowitz said.

But Tiara was out the door and gone. Americans move real fast, like they're allergic to staying still or something.

I wasn't introduced to the Rev "Two Churches" Horrowitz until later that evening—way after I'd got unpacked and used to the twin bedroom I would share with Derry.

Instead of us all going to the Presbyterian evening service, they'd had mercy and let me try to catch up on some sleep—jet lag like, you know—but I couldn't get any. The place was too new. And Derry and his mom were too god-damn noisy. Yadda-yadda. Derry was making a right racket about me staying in his room when there was a perfectly good empty room upstairs.

I'd given up trying to sleep and was set on getting dressed when the Rev, back from his service, walked right in on me. I was stark naked, but this great big hulking man, balder than an bald eagle, pays no mind, comes up and shakes me by the hand.

"Good to finally meet you, William," he said.

With one hand over my cock, and the other in his, I said, "Yeah, and you, but the name's Wil."

"Well, Wil, you can call me Pops."

I agreed, "OK."

And that was it; he bugged out and left me to pull my clothes on.

So that there's the Horrowitz-z-zs. The loving of two consenting adults had produced two dissenting kids. And hell, them racketeers were determined to try to love me too, protect me from the Beast in myself and others, but I didn't like the discipline, even if it was softer than back home. Discipline was discipline. Jesus. The word is too damn close to disciple for comfort, don't you think?

I had an American Dream that first humid night. I was spinning round and round on this record label—Eddie Cochran's "Something Else." Yeah, I was spinning inside a Fifties jukebox when someone lifted the lid off. I looked up. The Fonz loomed giant-sized above me like God. Yea verily Henry Winkler winked down at midget me and did his thumbs-up catchphrase, "Hey."

I liked Fonzie. He might have been a small Italian Taig in real life but in *Happy Days* he was cool. I listened to him tell me to, "Chill, Wil. Those Taigs Peter and Seamus man, they're not worth going to jail for. You dig?"

I dug.

"This is a new start in the New World. In America you can be an individual."

I can?

"I'll look in on you again. Happy days, my main man."

Happy Days!

The dream ended with this spinning reeling feeling and looky here, the first Heavy Metal track playing full-blast. Who sure was fine looking? Who was something else?

That girl, Teresa, of course.

I woke up after the dream but must have jet-lagged back to sleep.

That Monday morning I felt like Hey, you know?

The Fonz was right. This was a new place, a new time, a new opportunity. I could be cool, I could remake my rep. I had things I wanted to do in the U.S. of A.: like see Van Halen live from the back of a pink Cadillac wearing a Green Bay Packers helmet and stuffing a burger into my gob whilst getting a blow job from three naked sorority girls and Teresa. So, I decided to be positive. I wouldn't kill Seamus, at least not that day; hell the way I was feeling, maybe not ever if he'd apologize?

I got up and dressed in my own clothes and then I woke Derry up. "What's for breakfast," I said. "I'm starving."

Flapjacks and maple syrup was the answer. And Derry made them well tasty.

"Today's a Family Day," he said, with a gob full of mushed ook. "Do you ride?"

"What—a bike?"

"Bikes are for pussies," he sneered. "I'm talking about a motorbike here."

As a boy, especially a younger boy, it is nearly obligatory to lie when asked questions like these, but I was honest: "Nah. But I'm a fast learner."

In truth, honesty was the best policy because I'd thought ahead—what if I had boasted I could ride a scrambler and then when we got out and he said ride it dude and I hadn't a clue?

Derry took me out to the garage. It was stuffed to the gills with beat-up furniture.

"What's all this stuff for—bonfire wood?" I said.

Derry laughed. That was the first time I made him laugh. It was a strange sound, like it didn't belong to him. When he stopped, which was the nanosecond he became conscious he was laughing, he said, "Mom's an antiques dealer."

Derry wheeled the bike, or should I say iron horse, out of the back of the garage. It was a muddy-red Suzuki Scrambler.

"This is Suzi," he said and hopped on. He kick-started her. She blew this enormous fart of blue-oil smoke right in my face but I still fell in love with her—love for the second time on that trip. And what does love mean?—you got it, violence. "Get on."

I got on.

Derry gunned the engine. We took off, the three of us. What a ride! What a rush! Ripping around a circuit of the church grounds, the car park and the surrounding fields that belonged to the manse. We three simply were speed for those few minutes. Or at least I was. I should really only refer to my own world of experience. Derry must have raced that circuit a thousand times. In his eyes it must have seemed new only in that he was showing off his skill to a new guy on the block. And Suzi. She was just an iron horse.

The inevitable violence came later that morning when, after what I thought was a thorough lesson in how to ride and maintain her, I was allowed to take Suzi out on my own.

Derry watched over me as I kick-started her.

Derry told me again how to operate the gears.

Derry told me, "Go. Go. Go."

And I gunned her and then she was mine. And I was hers. And we were sheer acceleration around the circuit. First second third fourth. Brake. Fourth third second. Power on. Yeehaw!

And then I hit some mud in the corner of the field next to the manse.

Derry hadn't told me about mud and how to handle the slipperiness so I spun out, at thirty-something m.p.h., without a helmet.

I was lucky though. I got away with a few bruises and a long gash across the inside of my left calf.

Derry wasn't watching—he'd actually gone back into the house—so I had to limp Suzi back to the garage myself. I think I walked because I didn't have the confidence to ride her but it could have been that I thought she must be injured, I mean broken.

...

Suzi was broken, but not beyond repair as it turned out. My leg too wasn't broken, and we got that fixed a lot faster than the scrambler. I did however make the most of the injury when Mom Horrowitz returned from shopping, as is written in the boy genetic code of behavior.

Derry was not best pleased at my efforts either to ride or to be mollycoddled. He must have figured I was usurping his place in the household because he didn't speak to me for the rest of that day, preferring the company of the broken Suzi.

Mom Horrowitz told me to put my leg up so I watched movies until evening-time. One after the other. See, the Horrowitz-z-zs had cable. You could have all the movies you wanted. Nonstop movies. I love movies.

As if that wasn't enough movies, Derry had his favorite Sci-Fi movie on video. Cronenberg's *Scanners*. You know— the one where that guy's head explodes. Derry always said that bit was totally cool.

Phil phoned me later on that night. He was staying with Kuntz-z-zs in Waukesha, a neighboring suburb of New Berlin. He wasn't sounding too happy. He couldn't say why. He just wanted to come over. "Helmut is dying to meet you," Phil said sarcastically.

"And you've got to meet Derry," I said sarcastically.

"You mean Londonderry," Phil said.

"I wish I did!"

Me and Phil had a good laugh at that.

When we stopped he said, "Maybe we could all go to a drive-in or something?"

"I've watched three movies today already," I told him. "And you have to be able to drive to drive into a drive-in."

Phil laughed. He could always laugh at himself. That's such a rare quality.

"All right we'll decide when we get there," he told me.

Mom Kuntz (would you take this as your married name if you were a woman?) drove them over at about half seven.

Out in the sweltering twilight Derry met Phil. I met Helmut. We all shook hands, even though my first impression of Helmut was that he was a fatuous specky dickhead, and Phil didn't take a fancy to Derry's non-Blarney-charms.

"Where'd you get the name Derry then?" Phil asked. "Do you have Irish in you?"

"No," Derry said. "I'm all-American."

"With a name like Horrowitz?" Phil said back.

"Yeah!"

I chipped in. "Nah seriously, where did you get the name Derry?"

Derry shrugged. "My Mom loves Ireland for some reason?"

Loves Ireland—now that was an instant conversation stopper for us Prods. And just as well. See Mom Kuntz was anxious to be getting along—so we had to get into the station-wagon and decide what we were going to do quickly. It was

Derry who had a better idea than a movie. "Let's go down to Bluebelles."

Helmut said, "Yeah."

Phil asked, "We're going to a flowershop?"

"Get real," said Derry. "It's this ice-cream parlor. All the kids go."

"Including Projectees?" I said.

Helmut said, "Yeah."

I just stared at him, hackles a-rising. Helmut was definitely the end product of duh, years of dorks-kinder inbreeding. He spoke in this maddening monosyllabic monotone. What made it worse was that he hardly moved his mouth to make these uh-duh sounds. Helmut could never be remotely cool, even with a year's one-on-one lessons from the Fonz. I later learned he didn't even like Rock, let alone Heavy Metal. He was into Whitney Houston and Duran Duran. Jesus. And poor Phil had to live with him for a month. And we had to hang together. People would think he was our mate for fuck's sake!

But, his mom was our lift so we couldn't ditch him—at least until we got to this Bluebelles place—and not even then as it happened.

I stupidly imagined Bluebelles would look something like Arnold's out of *Happy Days*. Needless to say, when Mom Kuntz dropped us off in the lot, it didn't. It was this really tacky looking joint with blue and green neon signs and this big fake chocolate-fudge-nut-flake-syrup cone sticking out of its roof.

Their ice cream was good though. And pretty cheap too. I mention the price only because a hot fudge sundae was the first thing I bought with them dollars my Da bunged my Ma. It isn't anything to do with the Scots-Irish blood in me, OK?

"Better eat this fast," said Derry, "storm's coming in."

But what the hell, we stood outside, licking and posing with our cones in what must have been 80 percent humidity.

We looked about us. Other people were doing the same and feeling good about it.

There was nobody there we knew.

No Teresa to impress.

No Big Michael to make us feel small.

And mercifully, no Peter and Seamus.

But, wouldn't you know it, I was thinking my happy thoughts too soon—up pulled this pink Cadillac Coup de Ville and who should get out of my dream car but Seamus, Peter, and their American Fenian other halves. Bastards!

Seamus was staying with this ratty-looking nervous type, Merrick Stulz, whose big brother owned the Caddy. And Peter was staying with this small, hard-bitten wee fucker called Joe Shanahan.

They all shouted some abuse about fudge-punchers over but I didn't even acknowledge them.

Derry took it thick though. "Who're they?" he demanded.

I wouldn't tell him. I was too angry. So Phil simply said, "People you don't want to know."

"They're Catholics, right?" said Derry. "You guys don't like Catholics."

"Taigs is the right word," I said, impressed he knew even that much about Ulster.

"You want to fight them?" said Derry. His eyes lit up green. He was incredibly up for it all right.

In my mind's eye the Fonz and the Godfather joined us at Bluebelles to eat a dish best served cold: ice cream. "Not tonight—I'm chilling," I replied. "But I'll take a rain check."

"OK," Derry said, the wild Hulk-light going out of his eyes. He was David Banner again, only he'd still got all his clothes on, unlike the Doctor who for some non-reason was always left in that same pair of ripped jeans.

That happy day ended when it was young—like most nights in America. The days are too humid see, so that gives rise to these big thunderstorms at night.

It started to chuck down rain on us about a minute after I said the word rain check. We got into Bluebelles sharpish and Helmut phoned home for a ride.

I thought about my rain check as we looked out into the storm, waiting. I glared over at Seamus who was able to make a dash for the Caddy. He gave me the bird.

"He's never going to apologize, is he?" I muttered.

Phil just shook his head.

But Derry said, "Nobody apologizes for anything unless they're made to."

8 | CONCERTED EFFORTS

The Project let me settle in one more Family Day and then, on the Fourth of July, they took all us Projectees away for a two-day intensive concert rehearsal session at a residential resort.

I have to say the Family Days early on were kind of stupid in practice. You have to do stuff together to get to know Americans, either the stuff they're doing or like, joint stuff, because they're always doing stuff. That's all they know how to do. So, I hadn't really got to know the Horrowitz-z-zs at all. I must have clocked up a few hours inequality time with Mom Horrowitz, but the Rev was elusive. His congregations kept him well busy doing stuff. Tiara was always out with her girlfriends doing stuff. And Derry, well we did do some stuff together but he was sealed tight as a Lambeg Drum.

At the residential resort we were formally introduced to the Head Counsellor of the U.S. Project, one Stacey-May Roller. She was big and fat and always laughing and as black as coal. I liked her the moment we met—even though she was an authority figure and you could never say nah to her. I just tried to think of her as some local journalist by day and a lousy gospel singer on Sundays and a housebody at night because being such a lard-arse she couldn't have dated much.

The reason why I'm rattling on about Stacey-May so much is she was in charge of the concert we were to throw for the Americans the following evening. She had this idea wedged in her head that it could be a vaudeville gig, or as she put it to us, "A class variety act."

I told her one-to-one right at the start of rehearsals, "This is going to be a dead loss."

She told me, "Don't give me that pessimism, boy."

"It's realism," I said. "Honestly. I've seen this motley crue at work back home."

"What's real is people want a show tomorrow night and they're gonna get one. Now, Problem Child, how're you gonna help me?"

Stacey-May made me her stage manager, even though I was a Brit and it was the American Day of Independence. There was nothing I could do. I'd more or less asked for it. Me and my big mouth. I'd forgotten that the same rules applied here on vacation as in school or the UFF. Never draw attention to yourself. Never volunteer or put yourself in the position to be volunteered. I had been noticed. I had to pay the price even if it meant more embarrassment—which as it happens, it didn't.

Phil thought it was very funny that while they just arsed about all day I had to run around like a headless chicken getting the order of the Ulster and American acts right, the acts timed right, and keep ushering them on and off the stage.

"Hanging around doing nothing—that's the real chore," Derry said to me sarcastically.

What those two eejits didn't figure was that with the responsibility of leadership comes the privilege of power. I had the opportunity to talk to everybody, get to know the who's who of the American Projectees and win back some respect. I also got to break the ice with Teresa, who seemed pleased that I'd made some kind of effort to talk.

"I wouldn't have thought all this was your style, Wil?" said Teresa.

"Stacey-May says he's a man of hidden talents," said the American girl next to her.

"Have you met my host, Kelly Sticklegruber?" said Teresa.

"Nah," I said.

"I'm the hostess with the mostess," said Kelly. And boy was she right. She was a big girl with tits on her like a dead heat in a Zepellin race (one of my Da's ol' jokes). And I remember she had this tremendously womanly pear-shaped arse. I think I was so taken with it because it was the shape of a middle-aged woman's, a mother's if you like, but it had the rounded firmness of a virgin teenager. Yeah, Kelly's arse was one of my first sexual paradoxes. It was attractive and yet thoroughly repulsive at the same time . . .

Girls' bodies, see. They were just so, I mean, I hadn't got used to seeing them as, well, different. Back home it wasn't the same. You knew the girl from primary school. You'd called her names for years. Kidded her. Chased and nipped and tickled her. Whatever. But with girls like Teresa or Kelly or any new girl it was hard to know what to do and where to look and when to say the right sort of thing, if you could even think of the right sort of thing.

I must have done the right sort of thing because Kelly came off with, "We're thinking about having a midnight feast and you're now invited."

"Ta very much Kelly," I said.

"Thank Teresa," Kelly told me and winked.

I saw Teresa blush as Kelly pulled her away.

The other thing the stage manager job got me was a chance to have a crack at Peter and Seamus.

Phil gave me the idea to win Round Three. Firstly he said, I should get Stacey-May to put a comedy sketch together, you know, a basic two-man joke skit. So I did. And she liked the idea.

"Know anybody who could do it?" she asked.

"Well, there's a few jokers in this pack," I said, following Phil's advice.

"Uh-huh—"

"Peter Byrne and Seamus Finnegan are full of funnies but they're a tad shy."

That was all it took. Stacey-May got them to volunteer like she did to me. They were to script a comedy routine and get it ready by the next morning no excuses.

The rest of that day just dragged by. I had to get the *Sergeant Bilko* routine slotted in behind the Irish Dancing and the awful trumpet player and the *Gone with the Wind* skit, but it wasn't happening. Thankfully, at about three in the afternoon the counsellors broke up the rehearsals and started up the team games outside.

I saw the whole setup was to get you interacting with the enemy, showing you that they weren't that different, that you couldn't keep holding your age-old prejudices against them. The likes of Counsellor Ciaran couldn't fool me but I played along, at least for most of the day anyway. The other thing that didn't fool me either was why the Americans had taken us away to the residential resort on this day of all days. They didn't want us to see their nationalism-gone-rampant-jingoism, their military triumphalism, their victory parades—just in case we saw in them the reflection of our own.

Night fell and with it the sky—or so it sounded, what with another big thunderstorm. It totally washed out our chances of seeing any of the Fourth of July fireworks, not that we would have been encouraged to anyway.

Come ten, the storm had rumbled itself out and, after a late meal, we were all told by Stacey-May, "It's going to be a long day tomorrow so get some sleep you guys."

The counsellors then herded us like longhorn cattle into this big sports hall, where earlier we'd had to lay out our sleeping bags and stuff.

The good thing was that like cattle you could sleep-over with whoever you liked. There was no separation of the boys and the girls, just a stern warning not to get into the sleeping bags of members of the opposite sex.

The bad thing was that for a moment I thought that drover Stacey-May was going to bring her sleeping bag and bivouac over beside me, but thankfully that didn't happen.

Me, Phil, Derry and Helmut formed our own little camp not far from where Teresa and Kelly and Sorcha and some other girls were tittering and giggling. Gradually the noise died down and the counsellors were lulled into sleep.

At midnight we joined the girl's whisper-party. We brought along some candy. I gave Teresa this Hershey bar I'd bought earlier when me and Phil and Derry snuck away to a 7-Eleven across the street.

"Thanks, Wil," she said and pecked me on the cheek. Yeah, she kissed me and it felt good.

Whatever else happened that night happened in a sort of fuzz. See, I didn't get much sleep and my memory goes when I don't get enough sleep. I can tell you for sure I didn't get into Teresa's sleeping bag and she didn't dare go to sleep on me again.

9 | TIT FOR TAT

That following morning, listening to the snores of others, thinking about Teresa's kiss nearly drove me mad, but not quite. See, my own misplaced sense of loyalty became a UFF Court Martial, posing questions like—Was there such a thing as a good Taig? If I lost my hate for Taigs could I still be a good Prod? If I wasn't a good Prod then who would I be? Would my schoolmates still like me if I was seen to be different? Would my family? Would the Hit Squad? Could I go home if I had betrayed them? Was I a traitor?

Getting up and getting on with the malarkey of the day, doing stuff like an American, was the only way to put these questions to the back of my mind.

...

It was inevitable that over breakfast Phil and Derry would rib me mercilessly about the kiss. They hadn't had one, and fellas can get competitive about stuff like that.

"Are you going to see her?" asked Phil.

Now Derry wasn't to know the word "see" in the Ulster vernacular means "go out with," or "date," but he wasn't going to be left out of the cheap shots. "Are you going to pork her more like?"

I refused to comment on porking, preferring to munch my Kellogg's Cornflakes and fantasize about Teresa lying tits-out-for-the-lads naked on the hood of a pink Cadillac, beckoning to me, hand outstretched so I could see her gleaming Phi Alpha Beta whatever-they-call-them ring. I can even remember thinking—and this is scary—perhaps one *Porky's* sister would be enough?

Later on that afternoon, when the rehearsals were more or less sorted, I started to get paranoid again. The ol' doubts came back. If I lost my hate for Taigs who would I be? You could say, and my lawyer did at the trial, that's why I did what I did to Peter and Seamus. You see tit-for-tat is all the rage in Ulster. It happens most every day. An eye is taken for an eye, a tooth for a tooth, a kneecap for a kneecap, a life for a life. It is like some twisted form of dialogue between the two feuding halves of some split-up medieval family. The violence of our love for each other will not let us separate, will not let us divorce and move away to begin again. After all who would we be without each other? No one's.

And so, the need for revenge was strong within me. I needed to feel an identity. I needed to serve up some major ice cream.

Peter and Seamus had hammered together this dreadful, awful routine that was all about how St. Paddy chased the snakes out of Ireland. It was so cheesy the Americans would probably have called it neat, or cute, or something else inane. The problem with the pair of them was for the love of God they couldn't remember their lines. That's where I came in. As the stage manager I was in charge of the prompting pit and all the cue cards. You can imagine it, can't you? I know I did, about a hundred times before I actually, on the big night, in the middle of their skit, got their cards mixed up. It was a dishonest mistake, but to Stacey-May and the Projectees and the audience of patrons it still looked like a genuine arse-over-tits mistake—mainly Peter and Seamus's, of course.

There was Seamus in the middle of his speech and . . .

Oops, no more words.

A pause. Then I held up the wrong words . . .

Which he started to read . . .

Oops.

So he stopped.

And it was suddenly Seamus's turn to look mute and Alice Cooper *Hey-hey hey-hey hey-stoopid* in front of eighty people. Uh-duh.

To cover my tracks, earlier in the day I'd changed the numbers on the cue cards. Afterward Stacey-May and the counsellors read it as Peter and Seamus's mix-up. I, the hard-working Brit stage manager come-good, was entirely blame-less to them, but not to Seamus. When the pair of them died on stage I can tell you he held his arm out, made a gun of his fingers, pointed it at me and pulled the trigger.

As if you need to be told—he meant it wasn't over by a long shot. That's what happens with these feudal things. Tit follows tat follows tit and so on. The UFF teach you the only thing you can do is get your tit or tat in when the opportunity presents itself. Either that or you kill the Fen-ian fucker right from the off.

10   SHENANIGANS

The only other people to know what I'd done to Peter and Seamus apart from those two were Phil and Derry.

On a post-concert high, Phil waxed guitar-lick lyrical about it: "I'd go so far as to compare it to Eddie Van Halen's *Explosion* dude—it was perfect!"

Derry's praise was more . . . what's the word, understated. Words weren't used. There was just this change in his attitude toward me. See, Phil had told him a bit about what'd happened with Seamus on the plane, and so he knew what I was at. And I guess he must have liked the fact I didn't take any shite, even if I was small and annoying, because we got on better after that, not exactly like an American wooden house on fire, but better.

You know I really enjoyed the Family Day after the concert. It was a Friday if memory serves me right. Mom Horrowitz was out shopping with Tiara (where else would two women be?) and the Rev was out ministering to the needs of the chosen few. So what'd me and Derry do with this time and space? Not much in total. We sat around and watched a couple of TV movies on cable. We tried to fix Suzi together but failed. And in the afternoon—at Derry's insistence I might add—we discussed in some considerable detail why all Taigs should be hated because they're always trying to find out if you're a Taig, and if you're not, they act like you're one of the damned or something. I mean the lengths they go to just to find out—they'll speak to you in Gaelic, they'll try talking about the latest Hurley or Gaelic Games results, they'll ask you what school you go to, they'll even see how you pronounce the letter "H." I mean Jesus H. Christ!

Derry listened to me spouting off, and I mean he listened, took it all in, and then, when he'd had his fill of my love/hate he made us peanut-butter-and-jelly sandwiches. We gorbed the junk food in the kitchen and then for some reason we got to talking about the technique of necking girls with metal mouths (I think he was trying to boast about snogging a girl from his school called Anne who'd braces). When we'd finished arguing the pros and cons, and I definitely thought there were more cons than pros, he said, "You want to hear some Metal?"

"Yeah," I said. I could do a pretty mean impression of

Derry's "Yeah" by now. In fact, my accent was fast becoming the twangy-slangy, over-nasal nightmare of a Wisconsin native—or should I say a Wisconsin settler, because Americans aren't really natives of America at all. They're like us Prods in Ulster. Occupier-owners, who've stolen the land from conquered tribes like the Algonquin Indians.

Derry got this plain-sleeved record from upstairs and stuck it on the deck of the Rev's hi-fi.

"What is it?" I asked.

"Pops says it's sonic devil worship," he said, and cranked the volume up.

What was it? Black Sabbath with Ozzy of course. We started with *Paranoid* and head-banged our way through the whole album.

Later when we were both sitting down recovering from brain damage and stiff necks and fingers cramped by air guitar, the phone rang.

Derry got it, "Yeah?"

I could hear the tin-thin voice on the line. "Hi, is that Derry?"

"Yeah."

"Hi, it's Kelly from the Project here. Could I speak to Wil?"

"Yeah."

Derry threw me the phone—it was on one of those extended curly-cords so I just about caught it before it recoiled.

"Yeah?" I said.

"Wil, it's me Kelly. I'm throwing a pool party at seven tonight and Teresa and I'd like it if you two could come over? Say you will?"

"Who's going?"

"All the people we wanted to invite," she said.

"OK," I said.

11 | IN NATURE'S WAY

Come seven the Rev elected to drive Derry and me to the party in his pride and joy. "You like my van, Wil?" he said to me as we pulled out of the manse grounds at high speed.

"Sure do," I said. I think if I'd been honest and said, Nah, your van looks like a gay cream version of *The A-Team*'s, there was a strong possibility he would have pulled over and told me to sling my hook back to Ulster. Yeah, the Rev struck me as the kind of man who seriously dug his van. Woe betide any man or boy who slagged off his wheels.

"Sorry I haven't been able to give you guys much time as yet," the Rev said.

"That's OK, Pops," I said. "My Da never has any time

either." Yeah you're right—I was trying to give him the classic neglected son guilt trip. And he bought it. At that moment the Rev became the archetypal father figure who realizes how disappointing he is to the archetypal son figure and regrets all the stuff that could have been said or done better.

"I was just thinking," the Rev said. "How about I take you guys out for a burger at Rancheros tomorrow night?"

"How's about some range time too?" asked Derry, cashing in on the opportunity like a pro.

"Range time?" I said, trying to sound innocent.

"Shooting," Derry replied. "At the gun club."

"If you're sure he's up to it," said the Rev, nodding back at me.

"I am," I said. Little did the pair of them know I had already been to four UFF training camps. I had been trained by terrorists to live-fire a Colt .45 automatic and an AK-47. But I couldn't very well tell the Rev and Derry I was what Alco and the instructor called "a natural," could I?

"OK son," said the Rev. "Can do, if not tomorrow then real soon."

I hope you don't start thinking I was a manipulative kid or something because of what I did to the Rev. Or Derry either. It's the oldest trick us sons have. Every boy does it, or tries to anyway. It never worked on my Da until he and Ma got the divorce papers signed. I have to say them divorce papers gave me a lot of scope to manipulate him all right. If

I asked him for money he'd fork out, whereas before he'd just have given me the evil eye. Yeah, divorce may have turned my Da into a lousy good-for-nothing husband as Ma said but, he became a better Da out of it.

I have this theory that the change in his behavior was down to competition, unhealthy competition between him and my Ma for the best of my love. Da, the patriarchal animus of Ulster, just had to win, to try harder than he had before. He knew it was a losing battle but he'd fight to the bitter end just to spite her. See, boys always love their Ma best. It's practice for loving their mate later in life, isn't it? I was no different. I think it was Freud who said, "All neurotics are either Oedipus or Hamlet." Well, we know by now I was no Hamlet. Even if Da had died at the hands of a Taig I wouldn't have venerated him, and I sure as hell wouldn't have cursed Ma as a dirty whore if she'd married again.

We got to the pool party at eight. We were like the first and only ones there, which was cool because Kelly and Teresa made a right fuss of us.

Teresa even took me by the hand and led me in. In my Lights-Out fantasies, in the everlasting Void of my cell, I still remember and celebrate the tingle of her touch in my palm.

"Have you got your trunks?" said Kelly when we were poolside.

"We do indeed, like," answered Derry for us. Now, I want to point out that whereas he said this in his normal nasal Wisconsin twang, the syntax is straight from Ulster.

"Put them on here," Kelly said. "We won't look at you if you don't look at us." She stripped off her T-shirt and miniskirt and was suddenly almost bare naked in a bikini. I couldn't stop myself staring again at the curves and cracks of this motherly virgin's body.

"Kelly!" scolded Teresa. "You two can use the toilet to change. It's in here. I'll show you."

In most of the United States the legal age for drinking alcohol is twenty-one. The only reasons we were able to get drunk was because Kelly's parents had gone away for a night of "serious doinking" as Kelly put it, and Kelly's elder sister, who was supposed to be babysitting us, had gone out to smoke some dope with her jock boyfriend.

I'd been drinking since I was twelve so it was nothing new but I'd always heard that you shouldn't drink and swim. I was a bit paranoid about it.

"We'll not get cramps or anything will we?" I said.

"Of course not," said Kelly.

She was right. Not swimming would have defeated the whole purpose of the pool party so, we all ignored my warning. We gagged a whole bottle of Jack D. diluted with a whole two litres of Kmart diet cola between the four of us. Things were going great. I know it's soppy but the hard liquor and Teresa so near made me feel so warm inside I never even once felt the chill of the pool.

Teresa took off her sopping-wet white T-shirt after a few drinks. She slopped it on the pavement, laughed and said, "I wonder what the nuns would say if they saw me now."

Kelly told her, "They'd call you a slut."

Teresa just floated there in her bikini, laughed and then kissed me right on the mush, thrusting her tongue in to meet mine.

Needless to say that was the first time I had snogged or necked or kissed a Taig. It wasn't my first kiss by a long shot—I'd had a go at some of the estate girls back home—but it was my first real kissing session. What with all that hard-pressed tongue-knackering tonsil-hockey I felt like a man.

I got carried away. We both did. But not in the way you're thinking. See I didn't know what a gooseberry was, let alone that the other two would feel like that, all left out, you know, like? I wish I had, and then maybe Kelly wouldn't have made a move on Derry too, and maybe Derry wouldn't have said, "Get off, I don't want to neck with no Taig!"

"What did you just say to me, buster?" yelled hell-hath-no-fury Kelly and thrashed in the water.

"You heard me," Derry the Hulk shouted back.

"You called me a Taig." Kelly was nearly in hysterics. "He called me a Taig, Teresa!"

Teresa and me stopped necking. She cramped up just when I had my face in her neck and could feel her nipples like bullets on my chest. Taig you see. That just about did it. Derry sunk us but I got the blame of course.

I can't dispute it and won't now. Teresa's argument was sound: "How else would Derry know what the word Taig means, let alone to use it, if you hadn't coached him, Wil?"

What could I say? I felt like I was sinking, drowning in the pool. Alcohol and swimming and necking didn't mix. I should have listened to my own warning.

"The Project is supposed to be about peace and reconciliation, Wil," Teresa said. "These people are supposed to be teaching us how to live together, not the other way around."

"I'm sorry," I said.

And that's all I was allowed to say. They kicked us out. They threw our clothes out the front door at us and we had to leave, in our swimming trunks. It was only ten o'clock. We were drunk and honking of drink. We couldn't phone home for a lift. How could we explain what had happened? We'd have had to walk miles and miles to get back to New Berlin, in wet ucksters and everything; that is, if Derry hadn't come up with a scheme to get his sister to come get us.

See, Derry had this ace up his sleeve. That spring, while he was out on Suzi he came across his sister giving head to her current boyfriend in the fields behind the manse. Afterward he'd taken care not to mention blow jobs in their polite conversations, not even once, but that was because he hadn't needed to. I remember him telling me something like, "There's always a time when you need an ace to make people do things for you. Especially sisters."

So we phoned Tiara's boyfriend's house from a payphone. When it became clear Tiara was not going to come to collect us out of sisterly love, Derry dealt his ace over the phone, "If you don't come and get me I'll have to spit it out—like you did with Brad."

"You wouldn't," I heard her say.

"Try me," he said.

"You little shit," she shouted down the phone. "I'm going to get you for this, you little shit."

And Tiara was to be as good as her word. If only we hadn't blackmailed her into picking us up that night maybe, just maybe, she wouldn't have got in the way of our mission. Yeah, I can't help thinking that Derry's ace was *The Ace of Spades* for the both of us.

The day of mourning after the night before began with hangover hell. When we'd got in that night I'd dropped a dose of Paracetemol, but no joy. I was stuck with the pain. It seemed to come from my head, and my heart; ah, it came from all over.

I don't think it was the Jack D. that was hurting me though; it was because I had blown it, big-time. I just kept thinking that whatever was hidden behind the windows to Teresa's soul was gone, beyond my reach, and I would be left alone forever.

Over a late brunch, which for me was about a gallon of black coffee, Derry said, "I'm sorry."

"It's all right," I said. I didn't blame him. "Taig" was my

own fault, or so I thought back then. But I know now that that behavior, that sectarian defense mechanism, wasn't really my fault. It was my parents' fault. It was society's fault. It was love's fault.

It must have been getting on for two on that really seriously hot Saturday when Derry thought he'd help me out of it: hanging over the Void, that is. He brought me up to the empty room upstairs, poked about a bit under his bed and handed me a magazine. *Playboy*. And then he said, "Pull your pud. It'll make you feel a whole lot better."

I opened what we called a Dirty Mag back home and flicked through to the centerfold—who was incredible. Debbie, her name was. She had these melon tits and a heart-shaped arse to die for. And I think she'd shaved her golden pubes into a little come-get-it-here arrow too.

"There's some tissues in the drawer," said Derry at the door. "Just don't get the fucking pages stuck together, OK."

I had a wank as instructed. And it did make me feel better—once I'd cleaned up. I triple-checked Debbie for stains. There were none, so I stuffed her back under Derry's bed and went to find her secretive admirer.

Derry was out on the manse's back-porch drinking his mom's Kool-Aid. "Porn again," he said. "Have a drink."

"Thanks," I said and poured myself one.

We sat for a while and sweated in the sun, then he said, "You don't need her."

"Yeah," I said.

...

Porn again I was.

And I got to thinking I didn't need Teresa when I could have beautiful *Porky's* girls like Debbie anytime anyplace anywhere . . . ?

But then again, maybe that's not true. Nah, that's not right. What I'm trying to say is, I got to thinking I could have *Porky's* girls like Debbie anytime anyway anyhow . . . ?

Yeah. That's it. And what's more, I thought, I could have one of them girls without her permission. And even if I called her a Taig. And I could still be me too, so I wouldn't be losing or betraying my own sense of identity.

Thing is, what with all this thinking, and some more wanking that Family Day, I almost convinced myself, but not quite.

I'd like to say that I didn't become converted because I already knew that porn is the very representation of violent love, that it teaches you all the worst things: passivity, dissociation, objectification, projection, introjection, splitting, denial, mystification and sexual repression.

Yeah, I'd like you to believe that I knew all about these things and why they're the worst: namely, because they're the very intrapersonal and transpersonal processes that society uses to negate the experience of the individual human being. But, it wasn't that.

Thing was, I still wanted Teresa no matter how much porno jerking-off I did.

13 TWO CHURCHES

Services were the order of Sunday for the Horrowitz-z-zs.

I have to admit Rev Horrowitz wasn't a bad preacher as preachers go, but I didn't pay much heed to his sermonizing. Part of my inattention was to do with the fact that he was a Presbyterian and I was a Baptist and I didn't want him and his alternative religion messing with my mind. But in the main it was because I'd heard it all before. God is love. Yadda-yadda.

If I had known then what I know now I would have stood up and given the congregation my own sermon. It would have gone something like—Yeah, I agree God is love! But love isn't patient and kind like you think, it's group-minded violence. And religion is a protection racket just like the family and society. And the group mind, phenomenologically speaking, is God. And God's love is the violent love of the Father, the Patriarch. So rebel, sons and daughters of God, rebel against His love.

Derry didn't pay much attention to his Pops rattling on about God being love either. He was sitting next to me on the bum-numbing pew, half asleep. I had to nudge him awake to sing the hymns. He didn't like that but he got up to mime along with me.

When the first service was over, we were driven straight across New Berlin to the other church where Rev Horrowitz preached more or less the same service to that congregation. I don't think the second sermon about God being love and all carried as much conviction though because Derry actually fell asleep in that one and I let him sleep.

What can I say? I felt for him. Back home I've fallen asleep in church a few times but Ma always slapped me back awake sharpish. "The shame of it," she'd say. But Derry wasn't concerned with the shame of it when I eventually woke him up. His Pops was a Rev but he had no shame—or at least had learned to hide it so well that's what others would think.

That made me curious, maybe even envious, so I asked him when the service was over and the greetings were done and we were outside, on our own: "Do you believe in God, Derry?"

"No, but I've seen the Devil," he said. For a second he looked serious, dead serious, but then he added, "And his name is Ronnie James Dio."

That just about killed me.

It just about killed Derry as well.

We were retching with laughter by the time the Rev caught up with us in the car lot. "Was I that funny in there?" he said, not looking too amused at us.

"Nah," I answered back, trying to be instantly serious and failing.

Derry choked, "No, Pops, it's not you."

"What is it then? Share the joke, why don't you?" the Rev said.

"Nothing," said Derry.

"Must be X-rated humor then," said the Rev and turned away, looking disappointed in me.

I think it was a bit rich of him, don't you? Firing me the disappointed looks when he hadn't taken us out for a Rancheros' burger or a go on the range when he'd said he would. And all when we hadn't even complained once that he hadn't kept his word.

Typical Da—talks a good day out with his son but never comes through, never keeps his word. Women say all men are liars and they're right. Ask a son; ask any son where he learned to lie. At the feet of my father, the answer will be. You could ask Derry if he was still alive and he would say, I know he'd say, "Yeah, Wil, that's where I learned—at the feet of a Reverend."

...

Mom Horrowitz hadn't gone to the second morning service. She'd stayed home to throw together the only sit-down meal I had with the whole family, ever.

When we got back from church it was just about ready to eat and me and Derry, we were starving hungry for it.

The Rev asked me to say grace the way I would back in Ulster.

"Ta for the grub, Our Father," I said. "Amen."

"That it?" asked the Rev.

I nodded—that was my amazing grace.

"You don't stand on ceremony much do you, Wil?" sniped Tiara, trying to sound all important.

"Nah," I said.

The Rev shrugged and said, "OK people, let's eat."

Mom Horrowitz had half done up these big T-bone steaks for everyone, along with some mashed potatoes and grits and beans. It looked tasty but appearances were deceiving. The meat was totally soggy with blood. The vegetables were soggy with bloody water. You could tell Mom Horrowitz didn't have much practice at cooking real food. But give her a TV dinner anyday and everyday and she made them just fine.

"Even better than my Ma's," I lied to her. And like my own Ma she liked me lying better than if I'd told the truth. It was what she was used to.

Derry wanted us to go and try to fix Suzi again after dinner, but all that blood in the meat did something to my guts. Or at least that's what I think it was. I mean what else could it have been—an internal injury from my lost love? Nah.

Anyway, the blood kind of ruined that last afternoon of the first week in America for me. And what really ruined the evening to follow was two more church services on top of the infernal stomach ache.

God! Who says Prods never do penance?

It could have been that damn T-bone repeating on me but I had my second American Dream that night.

I was out riding Suzi, but not on the manse grounds, out on the open road, on the wrong side, buzzing along, when this big Harley cruised up beside me. The Fonz pulled down his aviator glasses and motioned for me to pull over.

I obeyed and he followed me onto the hard shoulder where I got off and leaned Suzi on her stand. I went up to the Fonz who quite clearly didn't feel like getting off his Hog; instead he just sat there, cool as you like in his leather jacket, and turned the engine off.

"Hey!" the Fonz said and took his glasses off.

"Fonzie," I said.

"How's things, amigo—as if I didn't know?"

"Lousy, Fonzie," I said.

"Lucky you have the Fonz to talk to then, isn't it?"

"Yeah, Fonzie," I said, keeping in mind that you have to keep saying "Fonzie" like you'd say "sir" to a superior officer, otherwise the Fonz can play rough.

"I've been thinking, about this Teresa chick—you can win her back."

"How, Fonzie?"

"All you have to do is say sorry—"

"I've done that—"

"Hey, always let the Fonz finish what he's saying!"

"OK, Fonzie."

"What I was going to say was—say sorry some more. Then say sorry one more time like your little heart was going to break. The chicks love it."

"You think that'll do the trick?" I said.

"Was I right or was I right the last time I gave you advice," the Fonz said and crossed his arms.

"OK, I'll do it, Fonzie."

"Hey," said the Fonz and gunned the Hog into life. "See you around, little guy."

The Fonz blasted off up the highway on the right side of the road.

I followed when I got Suzi started.

Then the dream just upped and ended.

...

I awoke with it still fresh in my mind on that Monday morning. I didn't feel sick anymore. I took on board what the Fonz had said. I would not give up on Teresa even if it meant begging.

After breakfast—those staple flapjacks and maple syrup—I asked Mom Horrowitz if I could phone Phil.

She said, "Don't you want to phone your parents, Wil?"

"What?" I said.

"Your parents—"

"Oh, yeah. I suppose I should."

Mom Horrowitz pointed at the phone. "Well, go on."

"I don't know what the time difference is? Ma'll kill me if I get her up out of bed."

"It's OK. They're ahead of us by six hours," she said.

"Right then." I picked up the phone and with Mom Horrowitz standing looking on, dialed home.

Ma answered after five rings. "Hello?"

I imagined her on the other end of the line, thousands of miles away, standing there in our hall in her apron.

"Hi, Mom," I said, and then corrected myself, "Ma, I mean."

"Wil, is that you?" Ma asked. "You sound so different."

" 'Tis."

"Ah, how are you, son?"

"Hanging together."

"Why didn't you phone sooner? I've been worrying myself half to death. I told you to phone me when you landed—and that was last week."

"I'm sorry. I got a bit carried away."

"Well. I suppose that's understandable. So, how are things going?"

"OK, Ma."

"Good. How's the family you're staying with?"

"OK, Ma."

"And your host—Derry?"

"Everything's OK, Ma."

Ma started gerning her lamps out. "You know, Wil, I miss you. Do you miss me?"

"Aye I do."

Ma gathered herself. "Phone me this weekend, Wil, yes? Now, could I speak to Mrs. Horrowitz?"

"No problems, Ma," I said and handed the phone over to Mom Horrowitz. I just caught my Ma's voice calling out "Good-bye, son" from thousands of miles away. Never was I so glad of the distance between me and her.

I got to phone Phil after my Ma'd had a comforting natter with Mom Horrowitz.

"Yo, Wil," Phil said when he got to the phone.

"Yo?"

Phil said, "It's what Stacey-May says instead of hello."

"OK. Yo. Wanna do something today?"

"Yeah, what?"

"Let's go to the Brookfield Mall."

"All right, dude!" Phil said.

...

Mom Kuntz (who Phil had nicknamed "Spunky Kuntz") picked us up and took us to the ultimate experience in American leisure—The Mall.

When Derry first said the word to me I pictured some kind of wild animal fight. You know like—maul, to be mauled by a wild animal, or like in the mauls and rucks of rugby. But nah. It was what we would call back in Ulster a "shopping centre": a very very big shopping center what with all the shops, an arcade, a bowling alley, and a cinema multiplex. And the only way you could get mauled in a mall was to go there on Saturdays when the women go shopping.

Anyway, it was like dying and going to consumer heaven for someone like me. No kidding. You see, there was nothing like this in Ulster at that time. The IRA had bombed the crap out of Belfast city center and any other town worth mentioning. And you didn't go shopping at what big stores were left in case you were caught in another bomb scare. That is, unless you were a woman, driven by those mothering genes to risk life and limb to gather up a few precious products.

First stop in heaven was, of course, Arcadia. And wow, there were so many games, so many machines, it was hard to choose which one to spend my Da's dollars on.

Rather than waste precious cents learning something new, I chose my old favorite—*Defender*. It was great. I was good at it. I beat Phil and Derry easily, one after the other, but even on a two-win confidence-high I could not beat

Helmut, the specky dickhead. Helmut was in short a *Defender* nerd. He slaughtered me. Such a trouncing was unacceptable to a fella like me who was brought up to win, to keep the enemy in their rightful lowly place so, of course, I demanded an explanation of his prowess. "Where the fuck'd you learn to play like that?"

Helmut told me with a maddening shrug, "This is where I hang out every weekend."

So much for Social Darwinism. So much for eugenics. And don't even talk to me about survival of the fittest. Ah well, they say everybody's good at something, don't they? Fair play to him, ol' Helmut's probably a computer programmer at Microsoft these days.

After we'd done the arcade and toured the mall, our next stop was the multiplex. All I can say to describe that is Zowee, dude. I mean like, you had a choice of movies to watch and huge buckets of buttered popcorn and big big bags of candy and mega-Cokes and staff dressed like style-clowns who wished that you'd, "Have a nice day."

Aw, and there was a photo of the Hollywod sign up on the wall.

It didn't take long to make up our minds on what film/movie to see. It had to be the biggie of the summer—*Aliens*—with your woman Sigourney Weaver.

I watched the Space Marines take on the Aliens and lose. I watched the Aliens lay their eggs inside the guts of the doomed Marines. I watched the eggs hatch and the Aliens explode out.

I thought about what it would be like to be one of those Marines, with an Alien gestating inside me . . .

"Wow, what'd you make of that?" said Phil as we left the credits scrolling away and came out of the darkness.

"I thought it was utterly cool," Derry said. "Especially the way the Aliens could spit acid."

"Yeah," added Helmut.

I was still lost in the thought, or should I say the memory, of the Aliens' self-administered cesarian births.

"Wil?" Phil said to me.

"It was the dog's bollocks," I said, "the way those Aliens burst out of them."

And so we all agreed it was a great movie. It's part of the unwritten code for teenage boys that you all agree, so we were all very pleased that we'd been given an opportunity to do so. It's also part of this code—which I shouldn't be writing down—that you conduct a postmortem of a movie, in every gory detail. So we did—over big frothy Milwaukee milkshakes.

By the time I'd finished noisily hoovering up the bubbles at the bottom of my cup I was getting bored of the gore-talk and got to thinking about the Fonz's advice and Teresa's phone number.

I left the others saying, "I have to go to the bog."

I had Teresa's number learned off by heart. I hoped it'd be her that answered but it wasn't. Instead, it was Kelly the Taig.

"Could I speak to Teresa, please," I said in my best false deep voice.

"Who's that?"

I couldn't say my own name, so I said, "It's Seamus."

Kelly said, "OK, I'll get her for you."

I don't know why I said Seamus. In light of what happened between those two and me it was such a dumb thing to do. But I named myself Seamus and Seamus I was.

"Hello, Seamus, how are you?" Teresa. And she sounded so friendly I envied that Taigy bastard.

"Hiya," I said in that deep voice which sounded nothing like Seamus at all.

"You sound like you've got the cold?"

"Aye," I said, forgetting Taigs don't use "Aye" all the time—the way Prods do to prove their Scottish descent. Aye—aye like fuck aye!

To which she replied, "Who is this?"

"Sure it's me, Seamus," I said.

But she wasn't to be fooled. "No, it's not. I know that voice. It's you, Wil, isn't it?"

I was set to say all my sorrys and then release the last sorrowful one like the wail of a banshee but the phone went dead so there was nothing for it but to go to the pissing bog like I said.

I didn't give up on Teresa. Derry gave up on me though, because the next day—a Family Tuesday—I phoned her, aw it must have been about ten times.

But no reply. She wasn't home, morning or afternoon.

I got to thinking—maybe if I thought about it hard enough—you know, really concentrated on saying sorry, it would somehow get to her. Yeah, I was so desperate I resorted to telepathy instead of telephony. Can you believe I sat on the bed in the bedroom for an hour in the afternoon, with the curtains shut, and tried some serious remote influencing, action-at-a-distance type stuff? I even refused Derry's offer of another day with Debbie. But then, can you blame me?

I was in love. And first love is all melancholic mystification coupled with violent possessive urges. Make-believe in
it and you can believe in magic. You can sympathetically see
yourself as a shaman, flying high above the streets of Milwaukee seeking out your beloved, looking over her, casting
a love-me-again spell on her. I know I did. I was that
shaman flyer.

It was Rev Horrowitz who shot the demon lover in me
down—

He came into the bedroom like an exorcist in a Stetson,
threw open the curtains and wrecked my spell of lust.

"OK, Wil," he pronounced. "It's five. I've cleared some
time. We're going out for that burger and some shooting."

"At Rancheros?" I said. The primal ambition to eat prime
steer burger and blast some targets took a hold of me. "And
the range—really?"

"Yep. Yeehaw. Get your hat on, son, and let's pony up."

That day, behind the wheel of his van, the Rev was a cowboy driver. Yep, yeehaw, on the way to Rancheros he gave
the bird to about ten different drivers. He was all, "Fucking
Ditwad!" this and, "Fucking Dork!" that and, "Why don't
you learn how to fucking drive, you pissant?"

All this from a man of the cloth. It killed me. Derry too.
You couldn't half see where Derry'd got the Hulk side of his
personality from. And sitting in the back, wearing a couple
of the Rev's old Stetsons we joined in the Rev's road rage
and gave them ditwad fuckers the bird.

That in turn, just about killed the Rev. "Amen, people," the Rev said. "Shouting, waving your arms about and gesturing a little is a great way to blow off steam."

I don't think it was, though. I heard the Rev died of a stroke a couple years after that, but then maybe, understandably given what we did, there was just too much steam in him to blow off by then.

I'd almost forgotten about Teresa by the time we'd got to Rancheros. You want to have seen this place. It was like a cross between a butcher's and a burger joint. They had all these skinned steer carcasses hanging in their windows and behind their counter. And then there was this huge fat guy, half butcher, half baker, there to serve you saying: "What'll you folks have?"

"Burgers," said Rev Horrowitz to the fat guy. "All you have to do is point, Wil."

"And then what?" I said.

The Rev was drooling as he said, "Then they cut some of that fresh meat out, grind it up, sear it and serve it to you."

So what else was there for it? I did what I was told, even though it felt weird pointing at the cow's arse and knowing I was going to eat it. "Where the legs meet the back-end, you know like?"

Looking every bit like modern day cowboys, the Rev and Derry pointed to spots kind of around the same area.

"Rare?" the huge fat guy asked me.

"Nah, well done," I said remembering Mom Horrowitz's T-bone none too fondly.

The Rev and Derry ordered theirs served up red rare.

While the huge fat guy picked up a knife and weighed into the carcass, we sat down at this big ol' pine picnic-type table.

I felt I had to ask, "What's the point in picking your own spot, Pops?"

"Here you get to know what you're eating, son," the Rev said. "In places like McDonald's and Burger King they serve you up all the minced scraps—you know like the eyelids, the ears, the chops, the cock and balls."

"Oh," I said, and suddenly my appetite for burgers just wasn't the same as it had been.

"Oh." That's what I said. And my appetite for destruction and over-consumption lessened. It was a matter of taste though, not of decency. See, if I'd been brought up decent— educated to know the value of every living thing in Mother Nature—the obscenity of Rancheros might have occurred to me. Who knows? I might even have been capable of compassionate thoughts toward all living animals, Taigs included.

I mean, for example, a shaman wouldn't have painted burgers on the walls of his cave, would he? Nah, that ol' horned and cloven-hooved shaman, he painted animals, the images of animals, so that he might gain power over that animal in the hunt the next day. I mean in the beginning man had to hunt down and kill his own food. And way back then if a hunter got lucky he respected his prey by offering up thanks to the animal's spirit and Mother Nature.

That couldn't be more removed from what I experienced at Rancheros. Gone are the days when you'd have to kill and to hack apart your own kill; machines and a few desensitized butchers do it for you. Gone are the days when we see animals as beings, or if you prefer, spirits, with experiences of their own. Gone are the days we thank Mother Nature for our kills—instead we believe that it's all rightfully ours for the taking. We are man, the prime predatorial species on earth. Nothing can stop us when we are made by our leaders to act together as a group.

But let me ask you a question, man—if you had to run for miles, stalk and kill an animal yourself every time you wanted to eat the luxury of Mother Nature's flesh, would you eat so much meat? I have to say that I'm a killer and that I wouldn't: even if, like a cowboy, I'd herded the prey animals together and kept them near me so I didn't have to run for miles before the kill. I'd rather eat fruits, berries, nuts, corn, wheat—whatever I could gather and grow. But then, that's why I turned vegetarian six years ago—not because I want to be awkward, like the Warden says.

Vegetarian-to-be or not, I ate that damn burger after the Rev said grace—even though it was totally rare with blood. Obviously "well done" meant uncooked in there. Still, I pretended to like it and finished most of it for the sake of the Rev's cowboy sentiments.

At the end of the meal, which was largely a silent get-it-down-your-neck affair, the Rev asked me, "Derry here tells me you're having a bit of love trouble?"

"Nah," I said, and shot Derry a dirty look.

"That wasn't why you were moping in your room today, was it?"

"Nah," I replied, "just a bit tired, you know."

"OK, OK. I can see you don't want to talk about it, Wil, but if you ever do, just say so, yeah?" It was then I got the message loud and clear that this whole trip had been some kind of mercy mission for me, that in the Rev's mind you only qualified for time if you were in need of his ministry.

"Yeah," I said.

"Well," the Rev sighed. "I've got to make a phone call here, guys, and find out if Mr. Hister needs me."

"Aw, Pops," Derry said, "you mean we're not going to the range?"

"No, son. I didn't say that. It's just that Mr. Hister is dying and he wants me to be there at the end to say a prayer for his soul, that's all. Who knows, the good Lord mightn't be in the mood for Mr. Hister's company tonight?"

As it turned out Mr. Hister died and the Rev couldn't take us to the range. Me and Derry were left with our hats on, disappointed by lies of omission again. But it has to be said I didn't mind so much—I was well used to it by then and my mind was otherwise occupied. The shaman in me just couldn't think of anything but Teresa and where she was and when I might see her in the flesh again.

If the shaman in me had been thinking straight—which is impossible because shamans think in spirals not in lines—then I would have known by the timetable of Project events that I would have only had to wait two more days to see Teresa—on the ill-fated Crystal River canoe-ride.

Once I did look at the timetable, those Family Days just dragged by. And what's more they were two of the hottest days in Milwaukee since records began. I mean, it was stifling hot and steam room humid. Those were the sort of days that could drive a man or boy mad, even with the air-con on full blast.

So what'd I do apart from go slowly mad? Well let's see,

for the first day all I can remember doing is drinking gallons of Mom Horrowitz's iced tea. That stuff'll really make you need to go to the bog all right.

And what else? You know, I don't rightly know where that Wednesday went? It's strange that amnesia, but I put it down to the way I'd kind of settled into the z-z-z routine of the Horrowitz family home. I'd become just another member of the family. I was Tiara's and Derry's temporary brother. I was Rev and Mom's second son. Things weren't new around there anymore and I wasn't either.

Truth was, I needed some action to take my mind off Teresa. My mind turned to what I did at home to feel free, to just be me, to knock boredom on the head. You know what I'm on about don't you? Yeah, you do. Like all young boys I terrorized my local neighborhood.

See, me and Derry just drank iced teas and pissed away that hot Wednesday but that night was a different matter. We were determined to stay out till way late—not past the Rev's eleven-thirty curfew, so's not to arouse suspicion—but late enough to do certain things: the sort of things I used to do every week back home when I was around ten and frankly, all of a sudden there, pissing my life away in America, missed like hell.

The good news was that Derry was up for anything I suggested. The bad news was that he had no idea what was entailed in innocent wee terror-games like Thunder 'n' Lightning. I had to explain the concept to him: "It's like this—you sneak up someone's drive and batter their door like thunder, and then you run away like lightning. Got that?"

"Yeah," Derry said. "But, there's this little problem, Wil."

"Really?" I said.

"That could get us shot."

"What do you mean?"

"Well, over here everyone's got guns."

"So?"

"So you can shoot a prowler on your own property and the cops'd call that self-defense."

"Nothing to worry about," I said. "We used to deliberately target the homes of SS RUC officers, and they'd guns to shoot the Provos."

Derry seemed impressed. "No shit?"

"Honest. It'll just make things more interesting, you'll see."

We were out on our first thunder of the night, halfway up the driveway of this big plush house on Elm Street that Derry said everybody in the neighborhood thought was haunted—and this security light comes on.

"I dare you to still do it," I whispered.

Derry was no chicken, that's for sure. Remember, this was his first time, and with me right behind him, he went up to that door and battered on it like King Billy-oh.

The both of us ran back down the drive to a hiding place where we could see who we'd summoned. Only neither of

us figured it'd be a demon straight from hell. I mean, this
guy spotted us in our hiding place from thirty yards away—
in the dark. And then, with a "Hey you!" he was sprinting
down his drive after us. There was no way I was hanging
around to find out what he was going to say. Derry neither.
We were off, haring down the sidewalk. Like lightning.
Two flashes of fleet fearful feet. The only problem was—
when I looked over my shoulder—this demon-guy had
more or less eaten up the lead we'd had from our head start
and he was still gaining on us, fast. There was no doubt in
my mind in that power-sapping instant—we were going to
get caught by the demon.

I guess Derry must have seen it that way too. He was up
ahead of me, faster than me, but he knew if I was caught he
would be in the shite too. The fear of that must have made
him angry, very angry, radioactive angry, because he
stopped dead right in front of me and stooped.

I mean, I nearly ran over him.

But I had the sense to keep running. "What are you
doing?" I said. "For fuck's sake, come on."

Derry the Hulk was hoking something out of a rockery
garden so he probably didn't even hear me. He certainly
didn't heed me. Instead, he turned to meet the demon with
a rock in his hand.

"I'll kill you, you little fuck," yelled the demon, who it
has to be said, looked a lot like Robert Englund.

But the demon was terribly wrong. You don't kill the
Hulk even if you're a demon. Nah. The Hulk just picks

something up—like Derry did—something like a rock—and throws it right at you—as Derry did—right into the demon's sneering face—into the mouth of hell.

There was a sound like the crack of doom and the demon fell from his great height. And then, a funny thing happened, something you'd say was straight off the TV. The Hulk stood there and roared down at the fallen demon. Roared and roared.

"Derry. Come on, Derry!" I said, running back for him.

The Hulk turned on me, yeah all green and nasty. I can tell you, I was totally taken aback. I expected to be propelled through the air with a roar of fury. But my fears were misplaced, he didn't roar at me. Not that night.

We got the hell out of that place. We flitted through the shadows until we got back onto the holy grounds of the manse.

"What are we going to do?" Derry said when we got to the back of the church. Gone was the roaring Hulk. Ol' Derry was shaking. I think he was suffering from a David Banner–type attack of conscience. "What am I going to tell them?" he was saying over and over.

I grabbed a hold of him by the T-shirt and shook him until it ripped at the neck. "Play it cool, Derry," I said. "We need an alibi so we'll go inside and hang around your mom for a while."

That freaked him out some more.

I slapped him around the gob. "What's done is done. You're going to have to hack this."

He looked over at the manse, shaking.

"Can you hack it?"

"Yeah."

And so we made Mom Horrowitz an unknowing accomplice to assault and battery and trespass and whatever else the cops might have charged us with if they'd ever caught us. They never did though. I don't know what happened to that demon we summoned. I had a few theories at the time, though they tended to revolve around stupid-arsed stuff like that ol' cursings and blessings thing again. But now I know better, I think that the demon's plush home and all was the result of some seven film deal, or other pact with the devil. Or that the demon—OK, I'll say it this once without demonizing him, that guy who looked like Robert Englund—had sins he really really needed to keep hidden, or else why didn't he go to the cops? Maybe he actually was a child-molester and killer, like Freddy?

When we got inside, a tired Mom Horrowitz didn't notice the state her son was in or his ripped shirt. She just upped and made us some hot chocolate and the pair of us, like good little boys, we settled down in front of the TV as ever. She was watching the ABC news while the Rev dozed.

Now I have to tell you, any news I'd watched in America up until then had been about America but, not long after we'd sat down, there was this bulletin on about the Troubles in Northern Ireland. I saw the SS RUC and Loyalists clash in a riot in the Tunnel of Portadown. And the IRA had let off a bomb somewhere in the Waterside of Londonderry. It brought it all flooding back. I suddenly remembered, it was the Eleventh Night back home. The Hit Squad would be out burning the Pope on the bonfires and letting off illegal fireworks and fighting the Pigs and hurling sparklers at each other and singing anti-Taig songs. Ah Jesus, it was the Eleventh. And where was I? Halfway around the world, lost, a stranger in a stranger land, being chased by demons not of my own making.

"I'll bet you're glad you're not back there tonight, Wil?" said Mom Horrowitz, looking at me with pity.

"You bet, Mom," I said, trying to fight the home-sickness of hatred so hard I didn't tell her where she could stick her pity.

" 'You bet, Mom'? " she repeated. "Wil, I do believe you have lost that lovely Irish accent of yours."

"Nah," I said.

"Well don't," she told me.

As if you could get rid of it that easy!

So now you know how me and Derry got our alibi. The price of innocence in the eyes of the law was high, though. I was the one who paid for it, the demonic crime. Did you know that the word "demon" predates Christianity—it means "one who knows" in Greek? Well, I was blessed and cursed to become that knowing one. I had to remember who I was. I had to remember what I had tried to forget. And I had to think about what that meant.

One waking nightmare of a question summed it up for

me. It seemed to rise like a hiss from the smashed mouth of hell: How could a good Prod like me have sunk so low as to fall in love with a Taig who didn't want to know him?

There was only one answer: I was a Judas.

Love and the Project had made me Judas H. Iscariot!

There was a big big storm that night. The thunder, it woke me up. Like Metallica I rode the lightning into the Twelfth of July.

17　JUDAS TWELFTH

Lightning, that cruel light of night or day, illuminates like nothing else on earth. What with all the excitement of America I'd kind of forgotten about Ulster, about who I was. How could I have forgotten so much in so short a time? How could I have become this all-American Judas?

I think, given perspective, I can answer that. Bar falling in love, it was all the Project's fault. See, its founders, they knew that who you are, who I was, all boils down to where and when you hailed from. Time and place. These are the two determinants, that's what our lives are all about. And they knew that by altering them, by taking me out of my place and time and projecting me into America, they'd alter me.

See, with Life—and I mean a whole life sentence—in another time and another place you or I could be someone completely different. Well, maybe not completely—but different enough. And you or I would never do the things that you or I did because you or I weren't you or I, that you or I. Either one of us could be a Hollywood movie mogul or a fisherman in Thailand or a lawyer or a banker or a nerd like Helmut working at Microsoft. We wouldn't have to be a terrorist fighting for the freedom of Ulster. We wouldn't have been brought up to be a murderer-in-waiting.

Time and place, they're our two fates.

Modern man, or boy, cannot escape these two weird scientific facts of fate. Your sociological environment acts on your genetic psychological makeup: it reacts right back, and hey presto, fate.

Want an example? I'll give you an example that's close to home. If your Da beat you up fate gives you two choices. Repeat the cycle of violence against others and revisit it on your children, or turn those violent urges back in on yourself—beat yourself up some more, why don't you? And why don't you? Because it's too hard. So you take it out on others, project it away from yourself.

That's what the Hulk and me did in the Thunder and Lightning of that fateful Eleventh Night. We took it out on others. And on the Twelfth of July in the morning, when I was lying dozy in bed, he was still a bit jumpy at what he'd done. "What if the cops come for us?" he said.

"Then we tell them it was a fight," I said.

"A fight?"

"We were out having a laugh. We did his door. He ran after us like a demon from hell. He tried to tackle me, started to lay into me. You fought him off with a rock. Self-defense."

"Self-defense, yeah."

"We didn't do anything wrong, Derry," I said.

"Yeah."

"It wasn't our fault."

"Yeah."

"So. We just sit tight, see what happens, OK?"

"Yeah."

Eating a bucketful of pretzels for brunch, we scanned the local and international news that Twelfth, Derry and me. Till high noon and beyond, we were flicking through all the stations, looking for a report on the demon. And of course, I was looking for reports on the Twelfth to get over this devilish homesickness that was rising in me.

There were no reports on the fallen demon; it was as if Freddy'd never existed and therefore no crime had been committed. Which was cool.

What was even better was that I did get to see a bit of the orange parades on NBC—until Derry interrupted it with a whisper—"He could be dead, you know?"

"He's not dead," I said back.

"How come you can be so cool about all this, Wil," Derry asked me.

"Been there, done that," I said, focusing in on a shot of the UVF Blood 'n' Thunder Band walking up the Lower Ormeau Road.

"What do you mean?" he said.

"Nothing," I said. I didn't want to blow my cover. I didn't know for certain that Derry would be right up for it; how could I have known for sure?

"Nothing," Derry said, impersonating my accent almost perfectly. "Something you mean?"

All I could see was the big parade come into Belfast City Centre. Drums banging. Flutes fluting and a-tuting. Banners wafting in the wind. The works. I could feel my body moving and twitching, in step.

"Are you going to tell me?" Derry said.

"Tell you what?"

"Tell me."

I saw the big dome of City Hall up ahead, in the distance. (City Hall has forever been synonymous with the favorite word of all Unionist and Loyalist Ulster: NO!)

"Nah," I said. "How do I know you can keep a secret?"

That was a calculated shut-up question; a boy's-own conversation stopper. I was saying to him—until you prove you're loyal I won't trust you. So, like a decent fella, Derry shut his gob and watched the remaining pictures of the parades with me while we were sitting there sweating in the heat.

"What is this all about?" he said after awhile. "This Twelfth thing?"

There was only one answer. It was straight from 1690. I started singing "The Sash": "Sure my father wore it in his youth, in the bygone days of yore, and it's on the Twelfth I love to wear, the Sash my father wore . . ."

Why didn't I tell Derry the whole Twelfth story? You don't just blab out all the things that make you you, even if you know what you're fated to be, do you? You don't just tell someone you're a terrorist, do you?

Nah. At least, not unless you're a Judas. Not unless you've become a shaman flyer, traveled through time and space, and come to a state of mind that exists beyond these things. What exists beyond these things? The nothing to be scared of. The Void.

18 THE CRYSTAL RIVER

My experience of the Void back then was slim. Generally I went with the flow like everybody else. I thought what I thought that other people thought, I believed in the pseudo-truths that I thought they believed in. My social programming did what it is supposed to do and stopped me seeing the Void—until Teresa. When Teresa walked away from me that first time on Crawfordsburn Beach she made me feel the absence of any real sense of group belonging. Suddenly I was alone. My being part of some imagined greater whole did not matter. I recognized I was lonely and longing. It was like when we met she'd bored this terrible big hole in me with her eyes, you know?

That big hole is what I call the Void. You don't have to use my terminology though. It has many other names, names empty enough to strike fear into any man or boy: the Abyss, the Heart of Darkness, the Pit, Hell. You name it for yourself when you feel it, or rather when you feel the lack of it, because it doesn't exist. It is the place you, the individual you, came from. It is the place you will go back to. It is nowhere, the everywhere nowhere.

I felt the Void all right, that Friday the thirteenth, being bussed up north to the Crystal River. Teresa made me. She sat up at the back of the bus with Kelly and wouldn't even look at me. What made the big hole even bigger was that she sat in front of Seamus and he was giving her the cyclops eye and me, the evil eye.

How was I going to say sorry? How could I in front of Seamus, let alone all those other people? I mean, they were all Taigs. It would be like apologizing to every one of them for being a good Prod. That was impossible. I'd have to try and get her on her own. Somehow.

I was sitting in the middle-left of the bus with Derry beside me and Phil and Helmut behind us. Nobody was talking much. Nobody was mucking about. I think they were all feeling my Void to some degree and people don't like to feel the Void, whether it's in their own experience or in somebody else's.

"Snap out of it, Wil?" Phil said after a particularly long and uncomfortable silence.

"Yeah," seconded Derry.

"Yeah, snap out of it," thirded Helmut.

Being slagged by the other two was OK, but Helmut, that was something I couldn't take. I mean, that specky dickhead was sitting there wearing what must have been one of Phil's Iron Maiden T-shirts, *Powerslave*, and giving me grief.

"Fuck off, Helmut," I said back. "At least I'm not wearing an Iron Maiden T-shirt just to be like Phil."

"I am not!"

"Are so," I said.

"Am not," said Helmut.

"Arsehole," Phil said, looking daggers right at me.

That put an end to it. I think that's when I first realized Phil was getting all protective over Helmut. I mean, wearing matching Iron Maiden tops was kind of telling, but acceptable, as long as they didn't have the same Eddie on them. And they didn't—Phil's was Eddie in a straitjacket, off the *Piece of Mind* album. But, when Phil called me an asshole, when he chose to defend Helmut over me, it made me think about the flight over Cleopatra's Needle.

We arrived at Waupaca's Crystal River Chain O' Lakes just before noon. The counsellors hurry-hurried us all out of our bus and assembled us on the riverside for a safety demonstration from the river instructor or whatever the old codger giving the lecture was titled.

Old Man River showed us how to put on our life jackets.

We were shown how to get into our two-man Indian-style canoes. We were shown how to paddle in time. We were instructed not to worry about drowning because the river was no more than three feet deep anywhere along the course we were to navigate. Finally, we were warned to fork left at the sign that said JUNIOR ROUTE—THIS WAY or we might find ourselves paddling all the way to the Atlantic, but by that time Derry and me were tired of being talked at. We were giving big Stacey-May some stick.

"Aren't you coming with us, Stacey-May?" I asked her.

"You got to be joking," she said. "I'm too big for one of those things."

"Aw come on," said Derry. "How do you know till you try?"

"I know," she said, laughing and slapping her big belly. "It's hard enough trying to get in and out of the bath of a morning."

That conjured some rather revolting images of Stacey-May naked, squatting and washing her big black lard-arse in the bath so I didn't engage in any further goading.

When the counsellors were quite ready, we were all allowed to pair up, get ourselves in the twenty canoes and push off, out onto the Crystal River. I remember that moment of letting go so well. The sun was high. The water, molten crystal. Never had a place name seemed more apt. Me and Derry just floated away . . .

Aw, I know reminiscing in the first person can lead to

sentimentality, but who says you shouldn't indulge in a nostalgia trip, that the letting go of sentiment hasn't its place?

That's all the above is though—my unreliable reinvention of how things happened—you know, that we floated away for a peaceful rites-of-passage kind of experience, but the reality was more a shites-of-back-passage type thing. Right from the off, everybody was trying to get a stroke going and water was spraying everywhere and canoes were capsizing and people were not drowning because the water was too shallow, but that wasn't the near-shitty-catastrophe. In a splash-duel with Phil and Helmut we almost lost our Derry-special packed lunch: the tuna, cucumber and mayo submarine sandwiches in our rucksack. It was that close, and it would have been a big loss because we were going to need all of that energy for our extended journey that unlucky-for-some day.

About a third of the way down the river there was a picnic area set in the woods on the riverside. The counsellors (minus Stacey-May) waved us in and we all landed our canoes, and got into our own groups, and got stuck into our packed lunches.

Halfway into our submarines, that was when the trouble really started. See, Seamus and Peter chose that moment to come over for a quiet word with me. "What about you, Wil?" asked Peter wearing a fake smile.

"All right," I said and continued eating.

"Just in case you're wondering, we haven't forgotten about the concert," said Peter.

"He wasn't wondering," said Derry and stood up.

"This isn't your business," said Seamus. "It's between us and him."

Derry moved into Seamus's face and said, "Says who?"

"Man—you reek of tuna!" said Seamus and took a step back.

"Oh yeah?" Derry said.

"So it's like that, is it?" asked Seamus.

"There's two of you," said Derry. "And there's two of us now. Don't forget it."

"Don't forget me either," Phil said.

"Yeah and me," Helmut added in his baddest voice.

Seamus looked around us all and began backing off. "We were just coming over to shake hands and you homos go and start it all off again. On your heads be it."

"Fuck you," said Derry.

"Fuck you too," chorused Peter and Seamus.

When I look back I feel a certain pride at the solidarity shown for me by my group. Yeah, believe it or not, I the arch-individual was once a valued member of a group of mates. But I also feel an indebtedness to the others in the group and guilt and regret for what happened next.

I know, I know, I shouldn't feel these emotions. I didn't ask for their help. They gave it . . . I was about to say freely, but that is not true. Because nothing is free in a group, in a we, in an us. I'm not saying Derry did it because I'd owe him, or Phil or Helmut. We were all just doing what Us boys do faced with the enemy Them. Bonding. Becoming a brotherhood.

Back at the lunch site though we were all just finishing our submarines off when, up periscope—we saw Peter and Seamus lurking down by the canoes. Or rather, Phil, our group lookout did.

"What're they up to?" I asked.

"Don't know," said Phil. "I think they're getting into their boat."

Derry had a look. "Yeah they're getting a head start on everybody else."

"But it's not a race," Helmut said.

That was true. It wasn't supposed to be a race. But there's something about competition that the male mind, especially the young male mind, just cannot resist. We as a group saw what Seamus and Peter did as a direct challenge to us. That, as it turned out, wasn't the case—they weren't intending to race us at all. We figured that out for ourselves when we ran down to launch our canoes.

Peter and Seamus had stolen one of our paddles. To be more specific, they'd stolen it from mine and Derry's boat.

"Fucking bastards," Derry said.

"The wee shites," I added.

We looked around, checking to see they hadn't lifted anybody else's. Nah, everybody else had two paddles. So, the theft wasn't just a challenge to a race, or the start of Round Four. It was more personal. It was a declaration of all-out war.

We could have lifted somebody else's paddle and taken off after them but we didn't. Derry and me just accepted that this was war and that men had to endure hardship in war to get a crack at the enemy.

"We'll show them Taigs," I said. "Even with one bloody paddle."

We launched.

Phil and Helmut too.

Now, when we set off that seemed to cue everybody else into action. All the Projectees and counsellors threw their lunch rubbish into the garbage bins and launched their boats.

What happened next is embarrassing.

We couldn't go very fast with one paddle, even taking it in turns. So everybody began to overtake us. And I mean everybody. All-girl canoes, the works.

The first ones laughed at our efforts to keep up with them so we decided to look more leisurely, as if we meant to be just about drifting along with the current. By the time the last canoe, that of Teresa and Kelly, caught up with us we were so casual-looking it was almost Fonzie cool. They paddled slowly by us.

I just said, "Hi." I didn't think it was a good time to say sorry.

Kelly blanked me but Teresa was looking over. I think I saw the flicker of a smile on her lips. That flicker offered me some hope.

When Teresa and Kelly had gone from view, I could see Phil and Helmut, who'd stayed loyally by our side, were getting anxious to be off at a reasonable rate of knots.

"Go on, you two," I said.

"You sure?" Phil said. "We'll hang around."

"Nah. We'll be all right," I said, looking to Derry for support.

"Yeah," Derry said.

"OK," Phil said. "See you at the bottom."

"See you at the bottom," Helmut repeated.

And then with a few tandem strokes they left us in their wake and disappeared around a tree-lined bend.

All alone we paddled on, Derry and me. It was hard going at first. We took turns paddling and this meant we had to keep shifting positions because it was easier to steer the canoe from the back seat. Both of us nearly fell in, nearly not-drowned in the shallows.

We took the stress and the anger that should have been directed at Peter and Seamus and hurled it at each other.

"Watch what you're doing man-dear," I told Derry when he steered us into a sandbank.

"Stop complaining and get out," he said back.

"Me get out?" I said. "You did it. You fix it."

So he got out and pushed us off.

"You can paddle now," he said when he got back in with soaking sneakers.

A while after that though, we both began to appreciate the peace of the river with no one else about. We could hear the birds in the trees over the clear clear water rushing and bubbling along. This'll sound dumb but it was like it had become ours and we had become its favorite sons; like it only showed its real crystalline, crystallizing beauty to the last ones to run its course.

Of course, that didn't mean we weren't going to kick the living shite out of those Taigs Seamus and Peter when we got a hold of them.

I still don't know to this day where that infernal sign saying JUNIOR ROUTE—THIS WAY was. Maybe we missed it because we weren't looking in the right place, what with winding Stacey-May up about her lard-arse instead of listening. Maybe we were lulled into a tranquilizing tranquility by the river? I don't know. But miss the junior sign we did. And that took us the long way down, through the adult part of the river, which was deeper and darker and full of big black rocks.

"We're in deep water, Derry," I said as we shot some rapids.

"Yeah," he agreed.

"I think we've missed our turn, Derry," I said.

"Yeah."

"Where do you think we are?"

"Wil, I have no idea."

"Do you think this channel goes to the same place as the other?"

"Yeah."

"Yeah," I seconded his hope.

...

It's at times like those that you can experience the Void. When you feel so alone you get this out-of-group perspective. You see how small you are. How little you know. How few people would care if you got lost or died.

We'd missed our sign, Derry and me. We were worried we'd get into trouble. But we shouldn't have worried that much. There are so many signposts in life, so many other people telling you where you should go. I'm kind of glad we went our own way; glad we one-paddled our way into the Void.

So what if the Crystal River showed us its darker side? Like Algonquins we rode its rapids and pushed ourselves out of trouble more than a few times. Yeah, we were scared because it was starting to get dark early and we didn't know what lay ahead, but it was new and it was exciting: the hardship of war and the terrible beauty of Mother Nature, that is. And, by the time we happened on an overturned canoe at another bar of rapids, we were even what I'd say was Void-happy.

All that changed when we saw whose boat it was.

There were Teresa and Kelly the Taig on the riverbank. Kelly just folded her arms and scowled at us, but Teresa waved timidly over and said, "Hi, Wil!"

"Hi," I said back. "Need some help?"

"Yes, please," Teresa said.

So a reluctant Derry and an enthusiastic me set about trying to salvage the sunken boat. It was no easy job. You see the way the boat had been wedged against the rocks meant that water was rushing over it, crushing it there. We tried everything but the river didn't want to let go.

"How the fuck did you do this?" Derry said to Kelly.

She shouted back. "I needed to powder my nose."

"What?" Derry said.

Teresa explained, "Kelly needed the toilet so we pulled over upstream and well, both of us got out. While she was behind a tree, I wasn't looking and the canoe must have floated off."

"Where are your paddles?" I said.

"They must have floated off too," Teresa answered.

"Floated off," said Derry. "That sounds like the stupid kind of excuse my sister would use for losing something!"

That created an awkward silence in which the only sounds were the rush of the river and groans of Derry. "We're not going to be able to budge this, Wil," he said to me.

"Ah well, never mind, they can come with us," I said. I felt a bit like El Cid, rescuing his Sophia from distress.

"No they can't. They'll sink us," Derry said. "And remember we only have one paddle."

We both turned to the girls.

"We have a problem," I said. "We can't bring you both with us."

"No problem. I'm not going anywhere anyway anyhow with those two," Kelly said to Teresa.

Teresa tried to persuade her otherwise. "Kelly—it's not like we have a choice?"

Kelly was adamant, so the choice of passenger was made crystal clear for us.

"Come on, Teresa," I said, pointing to our canoe.

"There's a house up there on that hill," Derry told Kelly. "Phone from there to tell the Crystal River about their canoe and maybe some day they'll pick you up."

"Fine," said Kelly. "I'll do that."

"Maybe I should go with you?" said Teresa.

But Kelly was in a full sulk. "No. No. You go on with your boyfriend. I'll be all right."

The look on Teresa's face. It would have killed dead things! Kelly had obviously overstepped the mark once too often with her put-downs so, to spite her, Teresa came with us.

We left Kelly as she ran off to the house on the hill.

Teresa felt bad about leaving her. I sort of did too. But Derry was as pleased as punch. "She'll be all right," he said. "There aren't too many things out here that'll tackle something as venomous as her."

The three of us paddled down the river as twilight fell and the air got all gray and bitty. Strictly speaking, Derry did the paddling. Teresa just sat up front. I was in the middle.

A brave while passed before I got the courage to tap her on the shoulder.

She half-turned to hear me out.

"I'm sorry about what happened at your pool party," I told her low so's Derry wouldn't hear.

She nodded, looking sad.

I said, "I don't think of you as a Taig, Teresa."

She shrugged uncomfortably. "I don't think of you as a Prod either, Wil."

"I want us to be friends again," I said, and put my hand on hers.

"Just good friends, yes?" she said, and withdrew her hand.

I think I heard Derry making puke noises behind us but I ignored him . . .

"I'm sorry," I said one last time—the way the Fonz said the chicks really loved.

It didn't work, though. Instead of kissing and making up, we became just good friends formally. The Fonz was wrong about apologies.

The hole in me got wider.

Yeah, it would be fair to say I went into freefall despair.

I wasn't long for falling though. Round the next meander we happened on an ol' landing where the rest of the Projectees were waiting in the yellow bus for us, all except Counsellor Ciaran, who was standing there on the landing with his hands on his hips. "What time do you call this?" he shouted at us. "We've all been waiting for you lot for two and half hours."

"Sorry," said Teresa.

"Where've you been?" Counselor Ciaran demanded.

I stated, "Someone stole our bloody paddle!"

Teresa said, "And Kelly and I had an accident."

That's when it hit him that he was short a Projectee. "Oh my God! Where is Kelly? Is she all right?"

"Yeah," said Derry. "She went off to phone for help at some house."

Our lateness ceased to be of such importance as Counsellors Ciaran and Kate and Stacey-May took Teresa to see Old Man River to find out where Kelly had ended up. I think because it was Friday the thirteenth they all feared that she'd been cut up in the house on the hill like in that series of slasher movies.

Derry and me got on the bus with all the others and were told to wait for news of the missing person. We needn't have worried, not that with our other concerns we were worrying that much. Fear was the last thing on our minds. Terror was the first—there was the matter of the stolen paddle to deal with.

After saying our hellos to Phil and Helmut, me and Derry and Phil and Helmut went straight up to the back of the bus, where Seamus and Peter were sitting tittering.

"What's so funny?" Derry said, standing over Seamus in the aisle-seat.

"You," said Seamus and giggled his head off, along with Peter and their hosts, Merrick and Joe, who were obviously clued in to the big joke.

"Why'd you take our paddle, Seamus?" I said, pushing my way in, past Derry.

It was Peter who answered from his window-seat, "In case we lost ours."

They collapsed into hysterics. They thought they were safe, see, among their own, sitting down there laughing at us. But they weren't. Because the Void of love lost was howling down into their faces. And I was that Void. Hitting down at Seamus as hard as I could, I made contact with his left temple and it was some bang I tell you.

What followed was total mayhem. Group violence at its most hectic. The whole back of the bus erupted into a flail of fists. I saw Derry turn into the Hulk and smash Peter's head off the window. I caught a glimpse of Helmut going down. I think I saw Phil rush to get Joe off his fallen host. I don't know how many times I was hit by Seamus (it can't have been many) or hit out at him. I don't know how many times I hit that fella Merrick. I just don't recall an awful lot about the fight. It was too fierce, too brief, and I was too devoid of feeling for there to be many memories from it. My main recollection was a sensation of satisfaction though. If that thirteenth was anyone's unlucky day it was theirs. Round Four was ours! We beat them Taigs into submission.

There was a lot of ill-feeling after the fight—between us and them; them being seemingly everyone else.

Of course the Project, especially Counsellor Ciaran, couldn't just leave it at that. The Rev and Mom Horrowitz were informed of our "disgraceful behavior" directly upon our return home and took the other side's lies as gospel. As a result we, the criminal brothers, were sent to bed without supper, and with our wounds, what little there were, untended.

Lying in my bed, alone in the night, I refused to think of Teresa. I would not dream of the Fonz either. There was only darkness in my mind.

...

The next day, when we got up with hungry-heads on we were told by Mom Horrowitz, "No breakfast yet. Pops wants to see you two."

"Where is he?" sighed Derry.

"Outside on the porch."

We went out to face the music. At the grill-door we saw the Rev was sitting in the wicker chair, reading the Bible.

He didn't look up as we came out. "That'll do. Right there," he said.

We stopped.

The music began. It was not Steppenwolf's "Born to Be Wild," but it was loud.

"I had a phone call early this morning. From no less than the Chairman of Project Ulster himself. What Bishop Clement O'Riley shouted at me went something like, 'Reverend Horrowitz, we are supposed to provide a strife-free environment for these kids to make peace in, not create another war zone. The Project has been compromised and I can't have the Project compromised.' Do you know what else he said?"

"Nah," we said.

"He said, 'Mark my words. There will be repercussions.' And then, he rang off. You know what that means?"

"Nah," we said.

"It means you'll probably be kicked off the Project."

"Oh," we said, or maybe that was just me.

"Look at the state of you," the Rev said.

I was tempted to say the only state we were in was Wisconsin, but I didn't. Instead, I looked over at Derry. He had a bruised chin and a swollen nose but that was it. And Derry looked over at me. I'd got out of it with a few scratches and a banged-up ear.

The Rev shrugged and asked us, "Boys. What happened?"

We told him in one voice, loud and clear: "They started it. They stole our paddle."

"You fought over a paddle?" the Rev said.

We tried to make him understand what the significance of the paddle was but we couldn't.

The Rev cut us dead. "What ever happened to turning the other cheek, Derry?"

"With those two I ran out of cheeks, Pops," Derry said.

The Rev sighed. "Normally, I'd ground you for something like this, son, but I don't think that's appropriate what with this being a holiday for Wil. You tell me, Derry—what should your punishment be?"

"Nothing is what his punishment should be, Pops," I pleaded. "We were provoked."

"You don't understand, Wil," the Rev said. "Derry isn't allowed to fight anymore."

"How can he defend himself then?" I said.

"With words," sermonized the Rev. "With love."

That struck me dumb, speechless dumb then. It strikes me as plain dumb now. The Rev—this man who ran around trying to help other people with their problems—couldn't quite get it that his son's love was violence the same as anybody else's, and that clearly Derry's problem was that he'd more love in him than other people.

"Tell me what you'll do to make amends," the Rev said to Derry.

After a bit of thinking Derry said, "Wash the cars."

"The cars! You wash the cars and the windows of the manse and the church, and you swear not to fight again, and that might just make me forget this happened. Yeah?"

"Yeah," said Derry.

"Do you swear?" said the Rev and thrust his Bible into Derry's stomach.

"Yeah."

"Then raise your right hand up, son."

Derry put his left hand on the Bible and his right in the air—like he was in court. "I swear," he said through gritted teeth.

We ate Frosties for breakfast and then had some flapjacks without the syrup. Then Derry went out to the garage. I followed. We got the soapsuds together and set to washing the Rev's gay-looking A-Team van.

"Why aren't you allowed to fight anymore?" I asked him with a sponge in hand.

"No reason," he said.

"Tell me," I said.

"Look, you don't have to do this, so why don't you go inside and pull your pud or something?"

"Because I don't feel like it," I said, and splashed some soapy water at him.

"I'm not in the mood," he warned.

So I threw my sodden sponge at him.

It hit him square in the chest. Boy, did that ever make ol' David Banner mad. The Hulk picked up the bucket. "I'll throw this over you," he roared.

"That's why!" I said running backward away from him. "Your temper. You lost it and really hurt someone didn't you? And they found out?"

"Yeah, so what?" Derry roared.

I smiled and came back toward him with my hands up above my head. "So nothing," I said. "I just wanted to know."

We were on the last of the manse first-floor windows, when Derry finally told me the whole of the Hulk episode: "I was suspended from school for beating up this bully. I broke his jaw, five of his ribs and all the bones in his right hand."

"Jesus," I said.

"And I spat on him afterward," he added.

I looked at Derry. He was expecting condemnation. "Nice one," I said.

Derry smiled at me and shook his head. "You know, Wil. Other people in school they think I'm a psycho but you, you, you're a strange little guy."

"What do you mean?"

"I guess what I mean is you don't look like much of a fighter, but you are."

"That's because I'm an Ulster Freedom Fighter, Derry," I said.

"You're a what?"

"You wanted to know about it the other night. Well, now you know. I'm UFF."

He looked long and hard at me. "You're saying back home you're a terrorist?"

"A Loyalist terrorist, yeah, fighting for Queen and Country."

He frowned. "How'd you get on the Project then?"

"Nobody else knows."

"Holy shit," he said, and smiled that crooked smile of his. "Like you say—nice one."

We did the church windows in an almost reverential silence. The quiet was nothing to do with God or the stained-glass St. Paul on the road to Damascus, or the Rev's rage even. It wasn't to do with nerves, tottering around on top of two beat-up ol' sets of ladders either. It was the kind of peace you can only have with someone if you trust them with a secret you would never have trusted another being with.

When we were almost done Derry said, "You think they'll kick us off the Project, Wil?"

"Nah," I said. "Their type'll just give us what they think is a good talking to."

"You reckon?"

"They're liberals aren't they? Liberals have to be liberal."

"If they kick us off the Project they'll send you home on the next flight."

"I know—and you'll be grounded until you're twenty-one."

We laughed.

We knew it could be our last laugh together.

That really killed us.

Later that day after we'd finished our chores, who should roll up into the church car lot but our appointed Project judge and jurors: Stacey-May Roller and Counsellors Ciaran and Kate.

Mom Horrowitz ushered both us and them into the dining room where she kept all of her best antique furniture. We were made to sit around the Amish table she'd restored and listen while the counsellors drank coffee and talked at us.

"Wil and Derry, if your motives for fighting were sectarian we have no choice but to remove you from the Project," Counsellor Ciaran said to us like the dirty Fenian he was.

We said they weren't sectarian. They were personal. We had our paddle stolen and then we were provoked by insults.

But the Ulster liberals didn't listen.

"If you called Seamus a Taig we can't allow you to continue on the Project. Did you?" said Kate, unlike the good Prod she was.

Truth is I don't really know what was shouted out in the heat of that fight, if anything, but, never to underestimate the power of denial, we said that was a downright lie and if Seamus had said it then he was a dirty no-good liar.

But the Ulster counsellors wouldn't listen. They went on and on at us.

Stacey-May didn't say anything until our other interrogators ran out of coffee and steam. "Wil, Derry . . ."

She left this dramatic pause so's she'd have our full attention when she tried to play her good cop role; instead my mind had wandered back to thinking of her trying to get her lard-arse into her bath. "Would you say sorry to the others at the ecumenical service tomorrow?"

If they said sorry first, we said.

"What about if both sides say sorry at the same time?" Stacey-May the good cop proposed.

All right, we agreed.

Wouldn't you know, the "ecumaniacal" service was at a chapel!

Mom Horrowitz drove us there in her station wagon. The first I knew about it was when we arrived at the chapel gates. I said point blank, "There's no way I can go in there."

"What?" said Mom Horrowitz.

"I'm a Baptist for Christ's sake!"

"Don't blaspheme," she warned me.

"Sorry, Mom," I said. "It's just Baptists don't go to chapel. We go to church."

"You have to go," Mom Horrowitz said like it was a threat.

"Or what?"

"Or else I don't know," she said.

"You don't understand," I pleaded, trying a different tack. "My Da'll kill me if he finds out I went into a chapel to worship."

"Then my advice is don't tell him," she said. "This is what the Project is all about."

"Nobody told me I'd have to go to Mass."

"It's for your own good."

"You could have fooled me," I said.

"Wil," she said, "we want you to stay on with us, we really do, but you're going to have to swallow some pride here, son, or they'll remove you from the Project."

What was I going to do? I thought about having to go home. I thought of the way Ma would look when she had to collect me from Shannon Airport herself. I thought of having to leave my closest friend and never seeing him again. I looked over at Derry.

He leaned over and whispered in my ear, "Let's just do it for the sake of doing it, yeah?"

"Yeah," I said, or sighed more like.

We got out of the car and met up with Phil and Helmut, both of whom had two big shiners each, but there wasn't any time for me to say anything more than, "You look like you're wearing eye-shadow the pair of you."

Stacey-May led the counsellors as they escorted us to the meet-up point—under one of those big signs proclaiming GOD IS LOVE.

That's where it happened, the making of peace. In front of God. In front of that chapel. In front of a frowning Teresa, my just good friend. In front of every Projectee and most of the Americans' parents.

Yea verily, on their Taigy hallowed ground they made us shake hands. They made us say sorry.

I went first down that line of six Taigs—yeah that's right, I didn't even realize Seamus and Peter's hosts and two others had weighed in. Six of them Taigs and only four of us—and we still whipped them. I walked up past them like it was a military inspection. You want to have seen the battered state they were in. I can tell you I enjoyed shaking their hands, squeezing their bruised knuckles that little bit too hard. We all said sorry at exactly the same time as agreed, that is until I got to Peter where I paused, and smiled into his beat-up face, and said like an English officer, "Terribly sorry, old chap."

Peter bit his busted lip and said, "Sorry yourself."

Seamus was last in line. He wasn't bruised on his face except for the one I landed over his cyclops eye. I waited for him to say sorry first. He waited for me to say sorry first. Another fight was in the air, you could feel the wanting of it. There was a moment of hush among the whole assembly. Nobody budged as their whole peace-making exercise ground to a halt . . .

Except for Counsellor Ciaran, who stepped up to us. "Say sorry, fellas, shake hands and let that be it."

But Seamus and I just stood there like gunfighters, staring each other down. I really didn't like the way he could look down on me.

Counsellor Ciaran said, "Come on. Everybody's waiting to go into church."

I looked at Seamus. "So—" I began saying, with no intention of finishing before . . . Seamus said the full, "Sorry."

Got him! Only then did I add the missing, "—rry."

I held out my hand in victo-rry.

Seamus seized it.

I squeezed his fingers as hard as I could.

He dug his thumbnail into my thumb as we shook.

People clapped us, would you believe it? The Americans, no doubt? They'll clap anything, especially themselves, their own efforts at mediation, their intentions made good.

As the others filed forward to shake Seamus's hand I watched Derry carefully. He didn't even look at Seamus in case the Hulk decided to make another public appearance.

Our group reformed at the end of this parade and walked into the chapel side-by-side with the Taigs in a show of "or else" peace. Yeah, we had no choice but to do what we were told. Do it, or else! Or else what? "Or else I don't know" is the adult's stock-in-trade reply. And what does that mean— other than I'll hit you or I'll ground you or I'll ignore you or I'll kick you out of my house or, ultimately, I'll crush your spirit no matter what.

...

We sat together at the back of the chapel, as far from matriarch Horrowitz and Teresa the Void of lost love, and as close to a quick exit as possible. I justified my choice of position to the others in a whisper: "Just in case we have to run outside and boke."

The others gave me this strange look. I now know that they were looking at me with disbelief. They didn't expect the same thing from this service as me. I thought it would make me want to hurl because I had been led to believe that Taigs worshipped God in something like a Black Mass, you know—with witches fucking the devil up on the altar—just the complete opposite of what I believed to be a church service. Surprisingly, the service was not like the Iron Maiden video *Number of the Beast* but very similar to the Baptist Communion one. And shock-horror, us Prods were not struck down by God's lightning for taking part!

When we crossed town and got back to the manse, the Rev had finished both his services but not his ministering, never his ministering. When we walked into the kitchen he was glugging milk out of a carton with the face of a missing kid on it. He asked us how things went. I knew the reason he asked us was to shame us more, to enforce our communal submission, to make us more obedient in future.

"OK," said Derry.

"You make it up?" the Rev asked with a mouth full of white ook.

"Yeah," Derry said.

The Rev raised his carton to us. "I'm glad you did the right thing," he said. "For both your sakes."

"The right thing," I sneered—not meaning for it to come out loud.

"You don't think that was the right thing, Wil?" asked the Rev, taking my words as a challenge to his authority.

"I don't know," I said.

"Oh, so you don't think that was the right thing! Well, what else would you have done to save your sorry ass?"

Mom Horrowitz said, "Pops?"

"Sorry for the ass," the Rev said. "But the question stands."

"I don't know," I said again.

"Well I do. I sure do. Do you know why that is?"

"Nah," I said.

"I'm older, wiser, and I pray to God."

"We pray to God too, Pops," said Derry.

The Rev looked over the two of us standing there, in defiance of him, the patriarch. He set his milk carton down. "I think the two of you better start praying right now," he said.

The Rev moved toward us like the way my Da did when he was going to kick seven bells out of me.

"You fucking hit me, Da, and I'll kill you," I yelled, putting my fists up.

Before anything else could happen, Mom Horrowitz stepped in between us. She told a hold of his hand. "Look, Pops, they've eaten a lot of humble pie today. People choke on humble pie."

The Rev glared down at his tiny wife. Then us. Then her. "Amen to that," he said and walked out of the kitchen.

Mom Horrowitz came into our bedroom later that afternoon with some milk and some chocolate-chip cookies.

"Trick or treat," she said, and put them down on the chest of drawers.

Neither of us got up for the something good to eat, so she came and sat on the bed beside me. "You weren't scared in there, were you?"

I didn't answer.

"He wouldn't have hit you," she said. "Would he, Derry?"

Derry didn't answer.

"Don't think too bad of your Pops," she said to us. "He just believes, like his father before him, that sometimes you have to be cruel to be kind, OK?"

Derry and me, we resisted talk, were silent. That is sometimes the only weapon left to beloved sons.

She put her arm around me. "Nobody will hit you here," she said. "I promise you that."

After a lifetime of beatings, and my own Ma ignoring it, how could I have trusted her? I said nothing.

"Wil," she said. "It'd be nice if we all said sorry wouldn't it, and forgot this ever happened."

"Like this morning?" I said.

"Yeah, but it'll be easier. We're family aren't we?" she said back and smiled a gleaming white smile.

I made no reply. In my experience there was no reply to enforced peace in a family, except for the son to say sorry.

She left the room with the words, "Eat your cookies, and then you can have a word with Pops."

When I was sure she was gone I turned to Derry. "Does your Pops the Rev ever hit you?" I said.

Derry already had a cookie in his gob. "He's tried not to."

"But has he?"

Derry spat some milk-and-cookie ook out. "Why do you want to know?"

"I just do, all right. Has he?"

"Yeah."

"When?"

"When I was smaller."

"With his fists?"

"Nah," Derry said. "Not like that."

I fell silent. With envy. Or remorse. Or self-pity. Or something.

"Yours does, doesn't he?" Derry said.

I didn't answer. That was my answer. The silence of the Void was my only weapon against my Da.

Jesus supposedly said, "I am the way, the truth and the light. Nobody comes to the Father except by me."

Jesus H. was a son once upon a time too. But never forget, Jesus was His Daddy's best boy. Jesus, like Isaac before him, had been taught he should be happy to sacrifice himself on the altar of patriarchy.

Before a TV dinner of humble pie we went to see the Rev in his study. It was one of the few times I ventured upstairs in that house.

He had the door closed so we would have to knock and wait for him to say, "Come in."

We went in.

"Sit down," he said.

We sat down.

The Rev sighed, "Well—"

Forced to, we said sorry first.

"I'm sorry too, boys," the Rev said. "I lost my temper. It's just that you gave me a lot of trouble . . ."

So there you have it; like good little disciples we sacrificed ourselves on the altar of patriarchy. When we were eventually allowed to leave the room I was fuming, like I was little Isaac stabbed through the heart by Abraham and heaped on the pyre, burning up on the inside.

"That's the last time," I said to Derry as we walked down the stairs. "Jesus."

"Yeah," he said back.

That was the last time we would play out the role of Daddy's boys. For ever and ever. Amen.

Or so I stupidly thought.

21 PRIMAL HOARDING

I think it was Freud who had this theory about the Primal Horde. If I remember rightly what he was saying was that civilization began when a band of sons, a simian brotherhood, took down the tyrannical patriarch of their Horde. Not before time, boys! is what I say—even though, that's when it was.

There was a big problemo with this prehistoric mercy killing—Freud said that by killing the Father these ape brothers made his hold on them stronger. See, the sons all loved him in spite of hating him, they all owed him the vital protection he afforded them from others. The guilt of their rising up, it killed them. And I don't mean they died laughing. See, due to this original sin of patricide, Freud argued the brothers were supposed to have internalized this Holy Ghost of the Father and passed it on, generation to generation. Therefore the ferocity of the primal Father figure will never leave us. He has become our vengeful God.

Do I agree with Freud's theory? Aye, I do like fuck.

And this time by saying that, I mean yes I fucking do.

A criminal brotherhood. The Metal Mafia. That's what the Project father figures, Tyrant Holdfasts every one of them, forged with their peace-mongering that middling Sunday.

Phil phoned us up Monday morning. He sounded none too happy. "Let's do something today," he said, dead quiet so's not to be overheard by the Kuntz-z-zs. "We've got to get out of this house."

"What about the mall," I suggested.

"Strike one," he said.

"Bluebelles?"

"Strike two."

"Where then?"

"Strike three. That's a turkey," he said.

"What are you on about?"

"Bowling," he said. "Although I'm mixing my metaphors up with baseball too."

"You're weird, you know that?" I said.

"Aye," he said. "Can you collect us? The Spunky Kuntz Taxi Service is on strike due to the fight."

"I don't know," I said. Then I remembered Derry's ace of

spades and corrected myself. "Yeah, Tiara'll do it. What time?"

"Eleven," he said.

I was the mafioso who blackmailed Tiara the second time for a lift. She'd just come out of the bathroom, face still dripping with morning water and moisturizer and God knows what else when I knobbled her.

"Derry and me need a ride," I said.

"Phone a cab," she said.

"What?" I said.

"You heard me," she said.

"Blow job," I said.

"You little Irish creep!" she yelled and tried her best to hit me around the head with her towel.

I ripped the towel out of her hands and pushed her back. "Let's get two things straight here," I said. "One, I'm not Irish. Two, we need a lift and you're it, or else."

"Or else what?"

"Or else—I don't know."

Or else I don't know: yeah I used the magic parental threat words to get us that lift. In protest against them, Tiara tried to use the Void. She didn't say a single word as we collected Phil and Helmut, but we didn't care. And she stayed silent for the rest of the journey too, which was just dandy. However, when we arrived at the bowling alley and were getting out I said like Phil would: "Ta Ta Tiara. See you back here at oral six."

It was meant as a joke but it blew the top clean off her Void. "I'll get you, you little Irish creep," she swore. "Just you wait!"

The joke was good, but the comeback nearly killed us.

Derry and me laughed.

Phil and Helmut too.

Tiara sped away from us like a drag racer.

"Ten-pin bowling rocks!" said Helmut as he put on his bowling shoes.

"Did he really say that?" I asked Phil.

"He did," said Phil. "And he's right."

"But there's right and there's right, and there's wrong and there's wrong."

"What?" Phil said, and added, "Now who's acting weird?"

But he knew what I meant. I wasn't just saying Helmut made everything sound uncool; I was saying Helmut shouldn't be part of our group but, because of Phil's new-found like of him, we'd do our best to tolerate him.

It is compulsory to try to change the names of individuals within your group when you're truly bonding. Programming the bowling computer was just the process for such a rechristening.

Derry had the advantage in this nicknaming process because he knew both how to work the computer and, unlike Helmut, got there first. Now, nicknames are always handed out in the reverse pecking order of the group. And being aware that the illusion of every man being equal under God does not stand the testing of a group, it should be obvious who would be bowling first.

"You're up, Helmut. Who do you want to be?" asked Derry.

"Tom Cruise," Helmut said.

That was beyond knockout funny. Derry and me were in stitches. Phil laughed at Helmut. Even Helmut laughed at Helmut. We were all in stitches. After awhile Derry recovered enough to say, "No, seriously, what'll we call him?"

It was Phil who said, "Purple."

I don't think I've ever laughed as much at anything. I mean, I just crumpled into the curve of the seat.

Phil laughed so much at his own joke he started crying.

Derry laughed so much he misspelt the nickname and had to retype it.

Helmut didn't get it though. "Purple," he kept saying.

Every time he said it we just laughed more. In the end I had to tell him to stop the rib-crushing convulsions. "Purple—Helmut."

"Oh I see." That's when it sank in, with a dorky grin.

When we'd recovered Derry said, "OK, Phil, what are you going to be?"

"How's about Re?" I said, but rePhil wasn't funny enough.

We all thought about it some more.

"Adelphia," said Helmut like it was eureka. (With hindsight, naming Phil after the city of brotherly love, where he died and was buried in 1994, would have been appropriate, but it just sounded ridiculous then.)

Phil came up with his own name soon after we stopped laughing. "Heron," he proposed.

"Heron," Derry said. He didn't get it.

I didn't get it either.

And you can forget about Purple.

"Phil Heron—'Fill her in,' " said Phil.

Then we got it. That was kind of witty.

"What about you, Derry?" said Helmut.

"Aw no, we're doing Wil next," Derry said.

"Willy," said Phil without thinking.

That was worth a laugh even though it was getting sore to.

"Fool," said Helmut. "Wil Fool—Wilful."

That wasn't.

"Wil-o'-the-wisp," said Phil.

Funny but no cigar.

"Wil E. Coyote," said Derry, and although it wasn't hilarious, he typed it in and it stuck. I became known as Wile E. Coyote in our group. I didn't like it. But I wore it. As things turned out, I didn't have to wear it for very long.

Derry stood there, looking at us. Waiting. He was ready for it. The name he deserved.

"Londonderry," said Phil.

I liked that a lot. But—"Nah," I said, "Derry's the Hulk."

And so he was.

...

Wouldn't you know, Helmut was a hopeless bowler. He threw his toady weight-Eight bowls way off target.

Phil was only slightly better, but at least he didn't take it seriously. When he released the Ten-ball he just shouted, "Gutterball." And sure enough that was where it went.

Derry now, Derry was one of those Fourteen windmill bowlers who make you look bad, all whoosh and swoosh, style and spin. And rightly he won three out of the five games.

I took the other two in spite of having to bowl a Twelve, and that being only my fourth time playing the game. See, they only got an Ice-Bowl in Belfast the year before and it was way too expensive for the likes of me.

So, now you know the score.

The bowling itself wasn't that important though; we all knew who was going to win. They say it's the taking part that counts and in the case of our group that was true. You see it was early days for us and we needed to do stuff to bind ourselves together more; that is if we were going to survive—which of course we weren't going to.

When you have four people playing a game of bowls it lasts a fair time and is worth the money, so by the time we'd played five, it was more or less lunchtime.

We took off our sweaty red and black shoes and were all set to hand them back—only there was no one behind the counter to hand them to. Whoever's shift it was must have been having a quick lunch break, or in the bog, but that was their loss. See, it was then Derry spotted a case of Miller beer behind the counter.

"Look," he told me.

The hoard was ours for the taking. And being as you have to take what you can get in this life, I was in like Flynn.

Leaving nothing but the aroma of our teen-feet behind, we were out of there like nobody's business. Out on the street we took turns running with the crate. I'm telling you, it was heavy, but you could just hear the rattle of those twenty-four bottles of cold fizzy gold inside and that kept you going.

Needless to say, our criminal brotherhood had outlaw beer for lunch. We broke that red, white and blue patriarch Uncle Sam's prohibition on under twenty-ones again!

On a nearby patch of urban decay that had grown wild, we hunkered down and divided the spoils. Everyone got a fair share, if not an equal one. And then, we all set about the manly business of getting drunk. But Helmut couldn't handle his drink; he had to go and get mindless legless eyeless bombed-drunk on two bottles. I've never seen it hit someone so fast or hard as Helmut. Of course that was a lot to do with the fact that he'd never touched a drop in his life before.

Helmut started singing "Wild Boys" by Duran Duran. It was sad, man.

"Shut up," we told him, but would he shut it? Nah.

Phil took him by the arm and told him, "Sing some

metal, man. We're all Metallers here. We're like, the Metal Mafia, man."

And that's where the name came from. It wasn't anything more sinister than that—unlike what the papers reported after the killings.

So Helmut heeded Phil and switched tracks like a juke-box, onto Judas Priest's "Breaking the Law."

That was metal so we all joined in. Head-banging and air-guitaring and chest-bouncing off each other followed. Yeah, it was a mental metal afternoon all right, until way later when it started to rain.

The pissing rain sobered us up—all except Helmut. We had to take him to a diner and pour coffee down his neck for an hour before he could stop giggling and walk unaided.

Two bottles. Jesus.

Anyway, at around five, Derry phoned Tiara and told her to pick us up outside the diner. The diner was a dodgy wee hole of a place, but it was better staying there than returning to the scene of the crime to hang around for a lift. I mean, we had left our shoes on the counter in the bowling alley—it wasn't going to take a criminal profiler to work out the Metal Mafia was the beer thief.

Derry had the bright idea of buying us all two packs of chewing gum each, and Helmut got an extra packet of mints, to try to get rid of the smell of drink. When Tiara turned up—half an hour late for badness' sake—we were all chewing mint like madmen. I'm surprised we got home in one piece. Tiara's eyes must have been watering with the heat of all that spearmint. I know mine were.

Or maybe, that was because I was something akin to happy? See, we killed the Father that day and we danced on his grave and pissed our own warm flat gold on his Holy Ghost.

If only we'd known he'd come back to haunt us. If only we'd read some Freud in school we'd have seen you can't kill God the Father. He's inside you. You can fight it all you like but inside every son is a father, inside every individual is a group, and inside every group is the pecking order of, if not the primal horde, then the criminal brotherhood of civilization.

Yeah, if you're wondering, we did get away with it. The drinking that is. Pops wasn't in when we got home, again. Mom Horrowitz had a headache or something and had gone to bed. And Tiara, well, she still wasn't speaking to us.

I got away with the other thing too—I blanked the Void right out with hazy remembrances of the Metal Mafia carrying on. Helmut was such a dork! We went to bed early and slept like the dead. I would not think of Teresa that night. I would not dream of the Fonz.

We wanted to hang out as the Metal Mafia in the mall the next day, but Mom Horrowitz got us up early and told us she had a surprise for us.

"What is it?" Derry asked.

"You'll have to wait and see," she said.

"But Mom," complained Derry. "We said we'd see Phil and Helmut today at the mall."

"Cancel it," she said.

"For what?" Derry said.

"You'll have to wait and see."

"Where I come from, Mom, you don't break your word to your mates," I said. "No matter what."

Mom Horrowitz shrugged her shoulders at me and then said, "OK, if you don't want me to take you up to Green Bay to meet the Packers, that's OK."

"The Packers," I said.

"The Packers," Derry said.

"Yeah the Packers," she said. "They're in off-season training but it's open to the paying public."

"Today," I said.

"Today," Derry said.

"Yeah," she said. "Want to come?"

Not knowing I would be spending most of my life in Green Bay I said, "Yeah!"

"Yeah," Derry said too.

"OK, we'll have some breakfast and then we'll drive up there."

This was all a major minus-guilt trip for Mom Horrowitz and I knew it. She was trying to make up for our run-in with the Rev all by herself. It was nice of her too to think about us but the problem was, she'd given us a major plus-guilt trip to think about too. I mean, how were we going to tell the other members of our new group that we had sold out, that I cared more about getting an American Football helmet as a souvenir than I gave a hoot about their feelings? We weren't, was the answer. I came up with a different plan while dressing.

Over breakfast—of flapjacks and maple syrup—we were to argue loudly about how best to betray our mates.

"You phone them," I told Derry.

"No way," he said. "You do it."

"No way," I said. "It's your house."

"Phil's your friend."

"Helmut's yours."

"Oh yeah!"

"Yeah!"

That's when Mom Horrowitz came in line with the masterplan and decided that there was room in the stationwagon for Helmut and Phil to come along.

I can tell you those two were mighty grateful to Mom Horrowitz when we collected them and hit the road, Jack. I took that as a compliment to myself even though later, I would see their gratitude as a terrible insult.

Derry sat up front with his mom while the rest of us mucked about playing Trumps in the back—I think it was a pack of motorbike cards Phil had.

Anyway, there isn't much to say about the trip because we couldn't be ourselves in front of Mom Horrowitz. It was a good three and a half hours solid driving to Green Bay.

And after three and a half hours of being somebody else, never mind a lifetime, I guess fellas can get a bit funny on it.

At the home of the Pack we got out, stretched and looked around open-mouthed like tourists do. Some guy came up to us and handed us this out-of-date program.

"Pretty impressive, huh?" said Mom Horrowitz, pointing at the stadium.

There was no arguing with her. The big green stadium dwarfed any football stadia I'd ever been in. I mean even Windsor Park, home of the Blues and the Northern Irish national side, was tiny in comparison.

"How many people does it hold?" I said.

"About sixty thousand," said Derry. "Soldier Field—the Bears' one in Chicago holds something like seventy or so."

It was and still is hard to imagine a group of people that big in one place at one time just to be cheering on their team.

"Wow," I said.

"Wow," Helmut said, trying to get in on the awesome act, even though the dork admitted he'd been there before.

First stop was the practice ground.

We watched all these Packers kick seven shades of shite out of each other, and the occasional one throw or run with the ball. It was fascinating; like spectating on a game of murderball or a microcosmic war.

Mom Horrowitz cheered at some of the big hits from Number 66. "All right, Beast!" she yelled.

The Beast was this black man-mountain who was the Packers' star defensive lineman apparently. You should have seen this guy: he destroyed anybody in his path. I had my camera with me so I took a stack of photos of him, and I mean a stack: I filled films with his violent sacking plays.

Derry thought it was funny me running around trying to get the best angle of the Beast and not get a face full of the fence which shielded the ground from fans. "Maybe hidden deep in Wily Coyote's genes is the will to be a sports photographer," he said.

Phil quipped, "The only thing that's hidden in Wil E.'s jeans is his willy."

I didn't think that was funny.

Helmut though, he thought that was so droll he slapped Phil's arse—

Now, I did think the arse-slap was funny, in a way different way, but I let both my reactions slide. Why? I had Beast photos to take, sports fans!

When the Beast's hits had all but decimated the rest of his team, the coach blew his whistle and ended the practice. The players all picked each other up, slapped a few high fives and each other's arses, and left the pitch. (So that's where Helmut got that move from, I remember thinking, and feeling somewhat relieved there wasn't something funnier going on.)

The others dragged Mom Horrowitz away to get a hot dog at the stand by the ground, but instead of going along I went to the exit gate to the field. I had a sudden desire for the Beast's autograph, see. And I got most of the team too, even though to this day, I haven't a clue who any of them were. I just ran around shouting "Oi, mister!" and shoving my program at them and, wouldn't you know, most of them signed it.

The last guy off the pitch was the Beast. He was kicking his yellow scored and dented helmet along in front of him. He mustn't have liked it when the game ended or something. Yeah, I could see he was singularly pissed off like my Da, but this was my only opportunity to get his mark, so I said, "Oi, Mister Beast."

The Beast did his best to ignore me and bent to pick up his helmet. It was then I saw that written on the back of the helmet was the number 66 with an additional red 6 sprayed on beside the other two.

"Sign this, mister?" I said.

The Beast looked down on me. "You sound strange, kid," he growled. "Where you from?"

"Ulster," I replied.

"Where the hell's that?" the Beast growled.

There was no point in saying anything other than, "A long, long way away."

"Oh," he growled.

"I came here to see you, Beast," I said.

"You did?—all right!" his ego said, and he signed my program.

"You need that ol' helmet?" I said as he walked on by.

"Yeah," the Beast growled, looking at me like I was mad.

I went after him. "It's just I want a helmet like that as a souvenir of my visit."

"Kid. These helmets cost three hundred dollars apiece new."

"Wow—I mean damn!" I said.

The Beast sighed. "I'll tell you what kid, I need a new one anyway. You got the money, it's yours."

"I don't," I said.

"Life's all about the dough, kid." The Beast shrugged and strode away taking the 666 helmet with him.

Of course the others took the piss out of me when I went over to the hot dog stand.

"What were you talking to the Beast about?" said Phil.

"His helmet," I said.

Phil nearly choked, and had to spit out a mouthful of hot dog before he could laugh.

"You were talking to him about Helmut?" said Derry, trying to redirect his Mom's attention from the dick joke.

Helmut didn't get it. "You were talking about me?"

"Nah, his football helmet," I said. "I wanted one to show the fellas back home."

It was that moment—when I would be least amenable to it—that Mom Horrowitz decided to offer me some advice. "You're shooting a bit high, Wil. Lower your sights and you'll be happier."

"Thanks, Mom," I said sarcastically. "I needed that."

Derry handed me my hot dog.

Phil, still sniggering, winked at me.

I bit down into that hot dog, hard.

Phil's wink turned to a wince.

Once we'd gorbed our lunch Mom Horrowitz took us to the Packers' Hall of Fame. She was as keen as the hot dog mustard to show us this tribute to a once great football team who had won numerous Super Bowls in the Seventies—not the team of Beasty-Boy nobodies I'd got the autographs of.

Outside the entrance of the Hall stood this huge, almost cartoonish statue of a famous—so famous he'd been left anonymous—quarterback about to throw. Mom Horrowitz sighed in front of the statue and then went to buy the tickets.

"What's this place going to be like, Derry?" Phil said quietly as we queued.

"If you like buffed trophies and rotting jockstraps, great," Derry said.

"Why's your Mom so keen to get us in there then?" Phil said.

"She was a cheerleader at her school," he said. "She loves football. It's how she met Pops."

"He played?" I said.

"He was an offensive lineman," Derry answered.

"Yeah," I said to him. "He still is."

The interior of the Hall of Fame was much as Derry had said: lots of glass presentation boxes containing gleaming silver and ol' moldy leather and light-faded archive photos of men long since injured, in nursing homes, or dead.

Mom Horrowitz, thinking we were kindred football-worshipping spirits and all, tried to be my personal guide around the place. The others left us to it. I pretended to be interested in her commentary until I couldn't take it anymore. "I have to go to the bog," I said.

"Oh OK, Wil," she said. "You hurry back now and I'll tell you about the Packers' second Super Bowl win."

I looked for the others on the way to the toilet. I saw Derry sitting on a stool in a corner picking his nose but I couldn't find Phil or Helmut.

Little did I know they'd be in the bogs.

I was standing there having a slash when I heard these groans coming out of one of the cubicles in the corner. I pissed on in fits and starts. The groans got louder. I couldn't concentrate so I gave up. As I was washing my hands the groans turned to grunts: it sounded like someone was having the shite of the century . . .

That's when I had this thought that someone could be dying on the pot like Elvis.

"Are you all right in there?" I said.

The grunting stopped.

What a way to go, I thought, and rushed out to get Derry off his stool.

"Come on!" I told him.

He followed me into the bogs.

We both saw Phil coming out of the cubicle, pulling up his trousers, all sheepish like.

"Was that you, Phil?" I asked.

"What!" Phil said. He was flustered and clumsy doing up his belt.

"I heard some noises," I said. "I thought you were going to die like the King."

"What?" said Phil. "The King. Ah right—the King. Nah."

That's when we heard the giggling. It was unmistakably Helmut's dorky giggling.

"Helmut?" I called out. "Is that you?"

"No it's me," said Phil. "Ventriloquism, you know. I've learned to throw my voice."

Derry went up to the cubicle door. He knocked. "Helmut," he said. "You OK?"

That's when Helmut chose to come out of the cubicle—the same cubicle that Phil had just come out of.

What could you say at fourteen/fifteen—other than what Derry did: "Holy shit, you're homos."

I turned and left the bogs.

Derry followed.

A mortified Phil came out into the Hall of Fame after us. "I can explain," he said.

We just looked at him like he'd grown two heads.

Mom Horrowitz came over. "Explain what, dear?" she said.

Nobody said anything more.

I mean, what could you say to two homos after you'd caught them at it? What do you know about homosexuality at fourteen or fifteen? Nothing if your parents have anything to do about it. Less than nothing if your school wants to stay in the business of brainwashing kids. All you know is disturbing playground rumors about never bending to pick up soap in the shower.

In that taboo instant Derry and me became a subgroup of the Metal Mafia, an Us of our own, and the other two became a Them. It was Us or Them!

With hindsight, Derry and me shouldn't have been so prejudiced, but we were taught to be that way from Sunday School up—they make a big thing of God the Father destroying the sinful Sodom and Gomorrah even if they don't say what the sin was.

"What's up with you guys?" Mom Horrowitz asked half an hour or so into the way home. "You fall out or something?"

Nobody answered.

"You know," she continued, "you should all just say sorry to each other if you did. Like my mom always used to say, 'You shouldn't let the sun go down on your anger.' "

Nobody was saying anything.

Until Phil broke the code of silence, "Did you know, Mrs. Horrowitz—?"

I thought he was going to tell her what had happened. That we'd been mates with a couple of arse-bandits. So did Derry—and it made him angry. "Shut it," Derry the Hulk roared at Phil.

"Derry!" Mom Horrowitz said. "What's got into you?"

The Hulk just glared at her.

Phil tried again. "Did you know, Mrs. Horrowitz—"

The Hulk roared again at Phil. "I said shut it!"

But Phil-him-in had other ideas. "Did you know, Mrs. Horrowitz—that I for one really enjoyed the trip."

Purple Helmut said, "Me too."

The Hulk somehow managed to contain himself.

Wily Coyote did too.

"Oh well," said Mom Horrowitz looking disappointed in her sons, both the permanent and the temporary. "I'm glad somebody did."

If Mom Horrowitz had seen Phil fucking Helmut up the arse in them bogs I think she'd have been a bit less tolerant about the whole thing than we were.

"I for one really enjoyed the trip!" Phil had a brass neck on him all right.

Now you might detect in my tone if not in my words, that I'm still not exactly a big fan of sodomites. My view isn't based on the prejudice of others though; it's nothing to do with religion or morality or society. It's based on prison experience. Green Bay Correctional Institution will give you a certain perspective on the gay thing. In here male sex acts are stripped of any and all romantic illusions. They just are what they are: instinctive, violent, brutal, penetrative abuses of phallic power. I mean, women may have been evolved by Mother Nature to take it, but you try nearly being raped up the arse in the showers and see how much you like it!

That's not to say that all guy-gays are bad and should be put in the gas chambers, or prison, and what have you. Nah. Only the group mind can condemn them. An individual must realize it's not their fault they're different. Again the fault lies with the Father. Maybe genetics will explain homosexuality better than psychology can at present but, if one in ten men overidentify with their mothers to the point of wanting to be fucked up the arse by their father, then I think I'm right to say that's another indictment of the patriarchal system.

Yea verily I say unto thee, patriarchy buggers all us sons up.

Some of us bugger back.

Some of us get totally buggered.

I know, I know, that's a crude way of putting it, but I've dropped my soap in the shower, and if it wasn't for a guard doing the rounds . . .

Having said all that, I can't say I haven't been tempted in here to act like the Father myself. I'm still a young man. Living without sex, living my teenage years and especially my early twenties as an intercourse virgin, has been tough as hell; you can get to thinking about sticking it in anywhere.

Sometimes in Isolation, and now I'm being brutally honest with you, I even think about Phil that way. But back then, as an archetypal homophobe—we got shot of those two fags just as the sun was setting. Derry and me didn't even say good-bye to them, so utterly determined were we to let the sun set on our anger.

I would absolutely not think of love that night. Not Teresa.
Nor Phil or Helmut. And stupid Cupid, ol' Henry Winkler,
well he could go and get stuffed!

The whole morning of that Wednesday Derry and me reacted
to Phil and Helmut being gay by pulling our puds over Debbie and other heterosexual porn lovers until they were red raw.
Of course, him and me did it in separate rooms, our own
Voids. We weren't fagomaniacs. And of course we didn't say
what we were doing or anything. We just took it as read.

You know, we hardly stopped for breakfast. I came six
times. On the sixth go though, my coming was like the spit-

ting of hot acid so I took that as a STOP sign. I'd reached my natural limit of exploitation.

In my experience anger is never very far from sorrow. And wherever they are, guilt is too. All these emotions needed to find expression in me after such a loss. But I wouldn't let them. I was in denial, see. I didn't want to be alone. Or more properly, I didn't want to feel so lonely. If it wasn't for Derry, for us being mates, and if it wasn't for Debbie wanting me, Debbie with her legs spread yearning for me, I think I would have fallen completely out of love with my life.

The Void.

The Void would have taken me.

I would have fallen. I so nearly did. I couldn't help thinking in vicious spirals—how could Phil have betrayed me, over and over, and then I'd think about Teresa, over and over, and then my mind would turn to my Ma and Da and how their love was just a bag of shite, and on and on, into an infinity of people abusing whatever trust I placed in them.

It made me so angry. Aw Jesus it did, and try as I might, I couldn't find a channel for this anger, this sheer human aggression that was roused in me.

Derry couldn't either. When I looked at him at breakfast I could see the gamma rays glowing in his eyes.

In my experience violence is never very far from anger. And after the blows have been struck, follows the shame and the guilt—depending on who does the hitting and how much of a conscience they've been programmed to have.

Mom Horrowitz had left us a note telling us she'd be back later and to eat the lunch of soggy tuna and onion and cucumber submarines she'd left in the refrigerator. The fish smell was a little too close to our own finger-stink so we passed on those and made some peanut-butter-and-jelly toasties. Then we settled down, each of us in our private Voids, to watch some TV. But there was nothing decent on, nothing but some crap HBO movie on cable, and a load of weather warnings about the 60 percent chance of tornadoes around Milwaukee.

"Tornadoes," I said.

Derry yawned.

"You ever seen a tornado?" I asked.

"Yeah." Derry got up to his feet and turned the TV off.

"What do you do if you do see one?"

Derry stood over me and shrugged. "Run. Get under-cover or underground."

"Have you had to do that?"

"Yeah. A few times."

I realized Derry wasn't up for talking about tornadoes—that he'd something else on his mind—so guess what? I shut up.

Derry lay down on the couch. After what seemed like an eternity in the Void, he asked me, "So what does a terrorist like you do?"

"Me?" I said.

"Yeah."

"Aw, just small stuff."

He wasn't looking at me when he said. "What—exactly?"

"Territorial graffiti. Punishment beatings. Burn-outs. And running the estate protection rackets of course."

"Tell me about a punishment beating you did," he said, his voice trailing off into something like a sigh.

I said, "Nah."

"I told you about mine!" Derry yelled. "Now, you tell me about yours." That was the first time Derry turned on me. I saw the Hulk flare green and nasty in his eyes.

"OK," I said. "OK. There was this one time when the Hit Squad—"

"The Hit Squad?"

"My UFF patrol. Me, Wee Sammy, Brian and Rick the Prick."

"Uh-huh."

"We were told to pay a middle of the night visit on this fella Johnny McIlwrath who lived on the edge of our estate. He was a UFF drug-dealer you know, only he was suspected of pocketing some of the takings from his deals."

"Yeah."

"So the four of us snuck out of our homes, got kitted out, and went around to his house—"

"You mean you had guns?"

"Nah. We had the usual tools. A twelve-pound sledge-hammer. Two baseball bats with six-inch nails knocked through the top. And everyone had to bring their own knuckle-duster."

"No knives even?"

"Nah, I told you. We just had the bats and whatnot. That's all you need. Anyway, we snuck around to his house and Rick the Prick knocked on the door real polite."

"Why didn't you just break the door in?"

"We always knocked real polite first time, that was the Hit Squad's trademark."

"OK."

"Now ol' Johnny must have been seriously bricking a visit because would he answer his own front door, nah, no way would he. So Rick the Prick knocked again—this time with the twelve-pound sledge. All of a sudden we were unwanted guests in Johnny's house, up his stairs, into the bedrooms and rounding up his kids and his bird and kicking his high-as-a-kite arse out of bed. Wee Sammy dragged him down the stairs by the hair. And we—"

I stopped of my own accord. There was something very wrong going on. I didn't feel right about telling my Terror tale. See the Hulk was sat on the edge of his seat waiting for it, waiting for Johnny to get it. And it was the Hulk, totally. There wasn't a trace of the David Banner left in Derry, just pure monstrous nuclear rage. In truth, I got scared, I choked. Maybe it was exposure to those gamma rays?

"You what," the Hulk roared at me.

"We beat him like we were supposed to," I said and walked out of the TV room into the kitchen.

The Hulk followed me though. "Tell me about the beating," he roared.

I turned and said, "Nah. I won't."

"Tell me!"

The Hulk grabbed my arm and twisted it behind my back.

"Derry," I cried. "Let go, Derry."

But the Hulk wouldn't let go until I'd told him what he wanted to hear. "We dragged him shrieking like a woman out into the garden. Wee Sammy and Brian hit him with the bats until he was nearly out. Then Rick the Prick did his right knee. That's it. Satisfied?"

"What did you do?"

"Held him down," I lied.

The Hulk tugged on my arm so hard it felt like he'd dislocated my shoulder. "The truth!"

I screamed, "I took the sledge and did his left. I did his left!"

The Hulk released me, ran out of the kitchen door and was gone.

I couldn't believe it. The utter bastard! He'd beaten me up when he was supposed to be my mate. The Hulk was no excuse!

I sulked in my room for a while, lying on the bed dead quiet, like I always did after Da'd hit me. Then with a start, I remembered about the tornadoes. A 60 percent chance of tornadoes! I jumped to, and went and turned on the TV sharpish. I just sat glued to the cable weather station. I felt it was going to happen before it did, see. The Void was coming for me. And sure enough, the forecasters issued a tornado warning for the suburbs of New Berlin and Waukesha at three o'clock.

I'll admit it, that got me scared. I was fourteen and home alone. I don't even think I really knew what a tornado looked like. I certainly didn't know what to do if a tornado touched down—Derry's words of undercover wisdom hadn't really sunk in.

I started looking out the window as well as at the TV; talk about keeping an eye out for trouble, that was me.

Did you know a tornado starts spinning way up in the clouds?

Did you know that it comes down like a finger from heaven?

I didn't.

Did you know that there is this strange calm as the finger stretches all the way down to the ground and then this roar as it hits?

I didn't then.

But I do now. See, that's what I watched happen slow at first; distant, off in the gray afternoon sky; then mad-fast.

The tornado touched down just outside the holy ground of the manse fields. It looked as though it was going to come the way of the manse.

"Derry!" I yelled. "Derry!"

I could say I shouted out of concern for my mate, even though he was violent toward me, but the truth is I was probably just calling for company. Someone, anyone, to face the roaring Void with.

Anyway, who should appear in the TV room door but

the Hulk? He roared and picked me up and ran with me out through the kitchen and down into the cellar.

In the underground gloom, David-Banner-Derry said sorry for what the Hulk did earlier. I said ta to Derry for what he did later. We left it at that. You may be thinking I should have been much more grateful to Derry, but as it happens, the Hulk didn't actually save my life. Like I said before— bravery and being a so-called hero is all about timing and placing, circadian rythyms, and biochemical reactions, but now you can add meteorological effects to the list of complicating factors.

See, when we ventured up aboveground, we discovered that the tornado, the Void, had lifted off before it came upon the manse.

Under the full arch of a glorious rainbow, a rainbow that seemed made for us two and us alone, we saw the only thing the Void had shredded was the boundary fence between what was holy and what was not.

The Fonz called me into his dream office that night. You know—the one in the back of Arnold's Diner. Yeah, I was a bit wary about going into the bogs after the Hall of Fame incident but I went anyway. You don't let the Fonz down, even if you're bogophobic and he himself has let you down with bad advice.

"Hey," said Fonzie, cool as you like in his white-tiled element. "Good to see you again, Wil."

"Hi," I said, deliberately leaving the Fonzie-sir out of my reply.

The Fonz must have decided to ignore my disrespect. He must also have decided to set aside his no-contact-with-the-leather rule because he put his arm around my shoulders. "We need to talk."

"What, about Teresa? Thanks to you she doesn't want to know me, except as a good friend."

The Fonz winced. "She used the just good friends line?"

"Yeah."

The Fonz patted me on the back. "Well, that's bad, but bad's not always as bad as it seems."

"Yeah?"

"Yeah," said the Fonz going to the gleaming bathroom mirror. "She isn't dating anyone else, is she?"

"Nah."

The Fonz whipped out his comb. "The next big Group Day's tomorrow isn't it?"

"Great America's not tomorrow but Friday."

The Fonz smiled and slicked his hair back with some water. "An amusement park—nowhere better."

"Yeah, Fonzie?"

The Fonz combed his hair back and said, "Yeah, Ritchie, chicks love to be scared as long as they know they aren't going to get hurt. What you've got to do is accidentally get in the car beside her on a roller-coaster ride."

"That won't be easy, Fonz, with Kelly hanging around."

"Try it and see," the Fonz said and put his comb back into his jacket.

"OK, Fonzie," I said reluctantly.

"I'll see you around."

I had to ask, didn't I? "Why are you helping me with Teresa, Fonzie?"

"Hey, you need a chick, Ritchie."

"My name's not Ritchie. It's Wil."

Fonzie shrugged. "You need a chick, Wil, or else . . ."

There was suddenly a bad smell in the toilet—I mean it was ten times worse than shite. It smelled like burnt meat, somebody who'd been fried and died and left to rot.

"Or else what—let me guess, Fonz, you're going to say—I don't know."

"Or else, Wil—one, two, Freddy's going to get you."

"Freddy—you mean the demon, Freddy Krueger?" I said, trying not to hurl with the reek and all.

"Yeah," whispered the Fonz and pointed to the cubicle. I could see it was occupied—the door was locked and there were two boots visible from the outside. "Your worst nightmare's in there, waiting to come out and he will, if you don't get to loving Teresa."

The nightmare ended abruptly—I remember waking up with a start to find I was sweating like a pig despite the chill of the air-con. And there was the taste of burnt flesh in my mouth. It was god-awful. I needed to spit it out or I was going to barf, so I rushed to the bog.

I spat and I rinsed with Derry's mouthwash, and I spat some more: I even flossed, but I couldn't get that taste or smell away for ages.

When I finally went back to bed I kept thinking of those

boots, those boots in the cubicle, and I wouldn't, couldn't get to sleep because it was when you slept that Freddy could get at you.

I must have dropped off and dozed at some point, but did I really sleep? Nah.

25 TOP GUN

Like I said before, I don't have a very good memory when I don't get a restful night's sleep. As a result the top of the morning following Nightmare 1's a bit hazy on it. It's funny when I think about it, ironic even—I can remember that dream as clear as day but not that day.

I've always wondered about that.

I looked into it on the Internet in the prison library. And you know what? Current dream theorists tell us that dreams are supposed to be analogies of the unresolved emotions of the previous waking day. That way, they say, your brain, more specifically your hippocampus, gets to de-stress itself while your body remains for the most part safely inert. But try as I might I couldn't find any working theories to explain what is happening when dreams become visions or portents.

Maybe only real shamans can know that?

I didn't tell Derry about my nightmare, or anyone else for that matter, up until now, but I took it seriously. I was going to try my heart out to get back with Teresa in Great America.

First things first, I have to tell you about having a nice day watching *Top Gun* with your man Tom Cruise and Kelly oops-I've-just-come-in-my-pants McGillis. Aw, what a great movie! Takes your breath away, you know?

Derry and me, not wanting to talk much in case we talked of the day before and fell out again, we went to the matinee at the mall multiplex. I was determined to savor the whole experience for the glorious fake it was. The Hollywood sign. The service with a smile. I bought extra buttered popcorn because of the atmosphere. It set me up to watch that movie twice. Derry must have thought I was crazy but it was just the ticket, see. Lots of testosterone-pumped boys with their Cold War toys and Maverick's ego writing checks his body couldn't cash, and romance, and shagging silhouettes and a rocking (albeit soft rock) soundtrack.

You just wanted to be Maverick, you know? He had it all. He could fly higher than heaven. He became a hero, saved the day, gave them ditwad Commies the bird. And he got the girl even though he couldn't sing a note. And to add to that, his hero Da was dead!

What more could any son in his right mind wish for?

I mean, so what if he killed his mate Goose? It's a war movie; you knew some tragedy like that was going to happen as soon as you found out Goose was married. In fact you knew it when you heard the name Goose—as in cook the, and wring the neck of . . .

When I look back on what I thought of that movie it makes me laugh.

It's no wonder I loved it because, like all Hollywood Blockbusters, it's made to a formula. That formula is based on what's called the heroic mythic journey. That journey is based on the way the Father would like his sons to behave on quests. Questing for the Father is much better than questioning him; it's easier too, so most sons go that way and become Daddy's boys. You know the story, you've seen it a thousand times. Daddy's boys leave their ordinary world when they receive his call to adventure; maybe they're a bit reluctant but a friendly mentor helps them see the light, and they cross the first threshold into the special world, where they encounter allies and enemies and are tested to see if they can approach the inmost cave. This is where they will struggle with death in a supreme ordeal and, if they survive, get the reward of the elixir of life which they will try to bring back to the ordinary world to give to the Father and his group.

Yeah, that's the way a hero is born to the group. Makes you feel all warm and cozy inside, doesn't it? That's because your own ego is forged from the myth of the hero. And

behind the sacrificial hero is, guess who, the legendary
Father, who through his representatives teaches: Do things
for your Da, it'll make you feel good. Do things for your
Ma, it'll make you feel good. Look after your brothers and
sisters, it'll make you feel good. Love your neighbors and do
things for them—that's the path of true happiness. When
you find someone to love, give everything you have in the
world to that person and, when the two of you have children which you must, give everything you have in the world
to them. Love your enemies—greater love has no man than
to lay down his life killing others for his country. Respect
the Law—it's made for your own good. Ask not what your
Queen/President can do for you but what you can do for
your Queen/President—you'll feel better about yourself. Be
nationalistic and socialistic because it'll make you feel like
you're needed, part of a bigger Volk, and maybe if you do it
really well, you'll feel like you matter.

Quest. Serve. Protect. Honor. Obey. Save. Sacrifice. Love.

All fired up, I left that multiplex five miles high in an
F-16 of an ego. I made my forced landing at a café in the
mall—the exact same one as we went to after *Aliens* with the
homos.

As there were only two of us, we broke the unwritten
code of boy behavior by skipping the movie postmortem
(we've covered that anyway). We had the Milwaukee milkshakes though.

"You all right, Wil?" Derry asked me.

"Yeah," I said back.

There was an awkward silence. I kept drinking.

"You're not still holding what went on yesterday against me, are you?" Derry said.

"Nah. Not so long as you swear never to do that to me again. Ever."

"OK, I swear. Are we cool now?"

"Yeah."

There was another gap. I was down to slurping froth, so I thought I better say something to fill it. "I was just thinking about Great America. You know—I've never ridden on a roller coaster."

"No shit."

"None."

"They have this latest one there. The Demon. I haven't been on it yet either."

"The Demon you say?"

"Yeah, it's meant to run half underground, half up in the air you know?"

"Sounds—" I got lost for the right word.

"—Scary? It will be."

26 GREAT AMERICA

We had to get up at the scrake of dawn and be down at the collection point for 7:30 to get the yellow Freddy bus to Great America. Mom Horrowitz drove us out of the manse at 6:45 but we had to go the whole way across the city, so me and Derry were the last Projectees there. Needless to say, we weren't very popular. We got booed on board. Mostly by Seamus and Peter and their Taig cronies at the back. But I think, out of the corner of my eye, I saw Helmut booing too.

While we were finding a decent seat, I looked for Teresa but I didn't see her. At first. She was there all right, sitting beside Kelly, except I didn't recognize her anymore. She'd had all her lovely blue-black hair cut off. I stood there staring in the horror, the horror, the horror, until—

Derry tapped me on the shoulder and said, "The only two-seater left is at the front."

"Aw fuck!" I said back, all the while looking at Teresa.

So we had to sit up at the front. That was uncool in itself, but what made it really uncool was we had to sit directly behind Stacey-May who had to have a seat all to herself. What made it unbearably uncool was the fact that Teresa had decided to model her looks on your woman Sinéad O'Connor!

I was still in shock half an hour into the journey when Stacey-May turned to me and said, "How you doing, Problem Child?"

"I'm hanging together," I said.

She looked at me intensely, like she did when she made me her stage manager.

"I'm not volunteering for anything," I added quickly.

"Did I ask you to?"

"Nah but you were going to."

Stacey-May shook her head and laughed. "You know, you're a mighty suspicious character, Wil."

Derry couldn't help but laugh too. "Yeah right," he said.

"And you're even more suspicious," said Stacey-May to Derry.

"Yeah!" said Derry, taking it as a compliment.

Stacey-May looked back at me. "I need two people, a boy

and a girl, for a piece I'm writing for the *Milwaukee Tribune* about the Project and, you're the boy for me."

I said, "Nah not today."

"I'm not doing it today," she said. "It'll be next Tuesday. At the group photo. OK?"

"I said nah."

"Yeah," said Derry. "He said nah."

Stacey-May smiled and turned away. That woman wouldn't take nah for an answer!

Forty-five minutes later, in a whole new state—that of Illinois—the bus arrived at the queue for the gates of Great America. I reckon it was nearly another hour before we finally got parked, and there were further delays waiting for us. Before we were let loose onto the roller coasters, every Projectee had to be given a free pass to get in, a free packed lunch, and a Rainbow of Hope T-shirt. Us fellas were told to take off our own T-shirts and leave them on the bus; the girls were told to wait and change after we'd got off. Yeah, fella or girl, we'd all be wearing the Project T-shirt that day so we'd be easily recognized by the crap red, yellow and blue rainbow print (easily controlled more like).

"Do we have to?" I asked Stacey-May.

She said, "Is the Pope Catholic, Problem Child?"

I decided for my own good I'd better not answer that question, or correct her terminology to something a little less politically correct.

With a hrmph I took one of Derry's hand-me-downs off

and put my own little rainbow on. Derry put his on too. And, looking like dorks-kinder, we went to have some fun.

Our free group passes allowed us access to every ride in the place. We thought that was just great until we saw the queues.

"Let's start small, work our way up to the Demon," Derry suggested. "And then we can do the big one—the American Eagle."

"Where first then?" I said, looking out for Teresa.

"We could do the White Water Rafting. That way we'll dry out by noon."

I saw Teresa and Kelly heading for the water ride. "OK, let's do that."

Derry saw who I was looking at and twigged onto my game. "You're not still after her are you?"

"Nah. Course not."

"Aye, the fuck you're not!" said Derry in the vernacular of home. "She's a Taig. And now she's a bald Taig. Forget it!"

He wasn't to know that I couldn't do that, that the core of my humanity depended on getting onto a roller coaster with Teresa and making her fall back into love with me.

The queue for the White Water Rafting was all of twenty minutes long and those were twenty long long long minutes I can tell you because guess who was two places in front of us?

That's right—Kelly and Teresa.

And guess who was in line right behind us?

Right again—our ex–brothers in crime, Phil and his Purple Helmut.

"Yo," Phil dared to say to me.

I looked away.

Derry and me tried to ignore them homos as best we could but—

"Yo, Wil," Phil said. "This isn't fair. I thought we were mates."

That was too much for Derry. He turned on Phil, the Hulk glowing in his eyes. "Not anymore, homo!"

"Derry," I warned him in a hiss. "Don't you fucking lose it here. Remember—you promised."

Derry somehow managed to bite back the anger and turned his back on the others. I had his back. "Listen," I said, trying to keep my voice low for all our sakes. "That was before, OK? What you did means you and I can't be friends, so just fuck off and leave us alone, OK?"

Those were the last words I ever said to Phil. I bitterly regret them. His black-eyed face just hollowed out as I spoke, you know? But what else was there to do?

There was room for eight on those circular rafts so we all got on the same one: me and Derry, Kelly and Teresa, Phil and Helmut, and two complete strangers. It definitely wasn't all fun and games at the start, what with Kelly love-hating Derry and Derry hating Kelly, and me and Derry love-hating Phil and Helmut and them probably love-hating us right back, and me and Teresa being just good friends, and the strangers hating us all because we were strange and there were more of us rainbows than them. I mean—if looks could kill, at the end of the ride they'd have found all eight of us lying sodden-dead on the floor.

But as the raft spun away down the water-shoot, I smiled across at the skinhead who used to be my eldritch Teresa.

She smiled back.

"Like your hair," I lied.

"Thanks," she replied.

"When'd you get it done?"

"Last Monday."

All you could hear was human silence. Rushing water. Nobody else backed me up with compliments like they should in that situation.

"Well, I like it," I lied again.

"Thanks," she replied again.

We entered into a series of tire-rapids and water splashed up into the raft. As his shorts got wet, Helmut shrieked like the big girl he was.

I smiled at Teresa.

She smiled back, all tight-lipped.

We spun toward bigger rapids and as we hit them, Kelly got drenched, and Teresa, she got wet.

Derry laughed for a full circle of the raft. But he stopped when he saw we were rushing toward the big double water-fall and it was our part of the circle that was going to get it in the spin.

The pair of us tried to paddle our way out of it but we were too close to avoid it and got absolutely head-to-toe soaked.

It was Kelly's turn to laugh at Derry, and Teresa's to laugh, politely, at me, and Phil's and Helmut's to be in vengeful hysterics at the both of us.

Phil and Helmut didn't have the last laugh though. They got hit with a big jet of water from a gantry, right at the end when they must have thought they were safe.

"What ride are you going on next?" I asked Teresa back on dry land.

"What ride are you, Wil?" asked Kelly, taking Teresa's arm and steering her away from me.

I looked to Derry for help. He shrugged and came up with, "The Meteorite?"

"Oh dear," said Kelly. "We're going to have lunch. Bye-bye."

They walked off.

I was all for going after Teresa but Derry said, "Leave it. We'll catch up with her later."

"OK. Let's have lunch anyway."

"OK," Derry said. "But you know what that means don't you?"

"Tell me."

"If we do go on the Meteorite next, we'll blow lunch-chunks all over the place."

So we went on the Meteorite before lunch just to please him. It was one of your whirlybird rides that spin the punt-

ers around and round, and holds them in place with only
centrifugal force and a piddling wee chain. It didn't scare
me as such, and it might even have helped to dry me out a
bit; I just really didn't like the head-spins it gave you after it
was over. When we got off and were standing still, I nearly
blew chunks even without eating my free lunch.

Derry thought that was very funny. "Let's do lunch," he
said.

The free lunch consisted of a bap filled with a cold knockwurst laced in German mustard and sauerkraut, a bitter
apple and my least favorite soft drink of all time, a Dr
Pepper.

Take it from me, it was as minging as it sounds. I barely
touched mine, much to Derry's delight. "Aw, don't you like
German food?"

"What's to like?"

"Shame. Give it here then."

He was to regret all that gorbing sooner rather than later.

Because I wasn't full of food I was keen to go on a roller
coaster right after Derry's extended lunch. I'd seen one
called Skyscraper which looked really interesting. It was
built in something like the shape of the iron-worked skele-
ton of, surprise surprise, a skyscraper.

"Let's do the Skyscraper," I suggested.

Derry rubbed his stomach. "OK," he said, not wanting to
look like a gutless wuss.

We queued for fifteen minutes and then we got into one

of the four-man cars. With the jingle of a bell the car lifted off, nice and easy, carrying us up and up and up around the outside rings of the ride. It was only at the top when things got hair-raising mad. One minute we were plummeting down, the next rocket-turning, the next spiraling, doing loops right left and center. It was intense. Like no other experience I'd ever had. I was clenched in a screaming position the whole time.

Derry unfortunately took screaming a step further—into grossness. On the upward curve of one of the last head-over-heels, instead of just sound, he added color to the mixture: totally chundering all over his head. (Thankfully not a single splatter came near my good self.)

"Fuck me," was all Derry could say when we came to a halt. Whereas I was in hysterics over his barfing and losing my roller coaster virginity, he was in a state of shock at what he'd done. That is until—

The guy from behind us yelled in our ears. "Yeah, fuck you!" We turned around to see what this guy's problem was. It was only then we realized the mess Derry's boke and gravity had made. I stopped laughing. The couple behind, a Hispanic duo, were plastered in chewed-up knockwurst and sauerkraut and Dr Pepper. The girl, who was picking bits out of her hair, started gurning her lamps out. The guy—who must have been about eighteen or so—grabbed Derry by the back of the neck. "I'm going to fuck you up real good ese."

"It wasn't my fault," said Derry.

"Leave them alone," sobbed the Hispanic girl. "They're only kids."

"What have you been eating man, this stinks!" the guy yelled at Derry but let him go.

I looked at Derry. "No Hulk?" I said.

He looked back at me, shaking his head. That's when I realized that Derry's fear-flight mechanisms were wired up different to his fear-fight ones. He wasn't always doomed to turn into the Hulk.

You don't need to be a genius to work out that the second those safety belts came off we were away like greyhounds out of the trap. There was no way that bokey guy was catching us, even if he'd tried.

We stopped our fear-flight at the bogs on the other side of the park. Derry went in to clean the barf off himself. I stood around. I thought about the hurling incident. And us getting away with it. And I thought about us getting away with what Derry did to the demon, Robert Englund. We seemed to be living charmed lives. That made me laugh, or snigger anyway.

You'll never guess who walked by as I waited outside, sniggering?

Wrong! Not Phil and Helmut.

Teresa. Without Kelly.

I called out to her: "Teresa!"

She came over.

I was all smiles, all charm. "Would you like to go on the Eagle with me?"

"Em—" she said and pointed to the Ladies'. "Not right now."

"Later then?"

She held her hands up. "OK."

"I'll meet you there at say, two-thirty."

She pointed at her left wrist. "I don't have a watch, Wil."

"It's one-thirty now and there's clocks all around the place."

"OK, two-thirty."

She rushed into the Ladies' just as Derry emerged from the Men's, completely soaking.

"What are you like?" I said to him.

"They were out of paper towels! Besides, people will think I got wet going on the raft ride."

"Yeah, if they don't smell the puke!"

He pulled his shirt up to his nose. "Do I still smell of puke?"

"Nah. I'm only kidding."

He did though, faintly, but that was OK with me. I'd have put up with him if he'd shit himself. I had a date, a real date.

It took forty-five minutes of queueing to get onto the Tidal Wave. The time dragged by. All the while Derry was so wet he looked like he'd been hit by a tsunami. I was actually beginning to think I'd miss my date when we finally got on board my first big roller coaster.

I made sure Derry sat on the outside. As we were clicked into our safety harnesses I said to him, "If you're going to puke again, lean out the side, eh?"

He glared at me, and the ride began. We shot off up and up and up this big rail which just ended mid-sky. My heart leapt into my mouth . . . Before we shot off the top though, like we'd seen in the queue, we just went screaming back down the way we came, past the starting point, and up another big rail which just ended in the sky.

My heart was still in my mouth when the Tidal Wave stopped. And I think I actually split the corners of my mouth what with screaming so much.

I made my date with two minutes to spare basically because Derry and me ran the whole way from the Tidal Wave to the biggest wooden roller coaster in America, the American Eagle.

Teresa wasn't there.

Judging by the signs, the queue was thirty minutes long. I waited around at the end of it for her until two-thirty when Derry said, "Join the queue. She can join you when she comes—if she comes."

"She's coming," I told him.

We joined the queue.

Five minutes passed. All around us the people were ogling the ride and getting scared way in advance like they were supposed to.

"You can feel their fear," Derry said—almost as if it was

the first time he'd ever felt that ol' hackle-raising tingle off a load of fatuous people.

"When she comes, make yourself scarce," I said.

"What?" he said.

"I want to ride the Eagle with her."

"No problem," he said with a tut. "I'll just make myself scarce."

Ten minutes passed as Derry sulked in the queue.

Twenty.

"Looks like you'll be riding the Eagle with me after all!" Derry gloated.

That was when I saw Teresa waving at the back of the queue.

"Come on," I yelled to her. "I've kept you a place!"

Unfortunately, I hadn't seen Seamus beside her. They both bunked the queue and took places behind us.

"What's he doing here, Teresa?" I asked.

"I'm escorting her, Wil," said Seamus. "Like a real gentleman."

"Really—and what would you know about that, Seamus?"

"I'll show you," Seamus said.

That's when he kissed her. And she kissed him back. Right in front of me.

Derry tried to stop me but I was reeling watching them. All my dreams of romance and blow jobs on the hood of a pink Cadillac went up in smoke before my tearing eyes. I'd lost her. "Don't, Wil!" I kind of heard Derry say. But the

Alien in me erupted out of my guts and had Seamus by the balls before anybody, including me, really even knew what was happening.

"Fuck!" squealed Seamus as the Alien in me applied fearsome pressure.

"Wil?" Derry said. "This isn't a good idea."

"Back off, Derry," I said. "This is my business!"

"Let him go, Wil!" shouted Teresa, all angry and shocked—like I was with her.

"I hope you like eunuchs, Teresa," I said. "Because I'm going to break his fucking balls."

"You're a fucking homo!" yelled Seamus and grabbed me by the neck.

I redoubled the pressure and he let go. I could see the sickening helplessness in his eyes. I felt strong. I felt like doing what the Godfather would do to a Mafia stool pigeon—tearing off his cock and balls and shoving them into his Taigy gob.

"Wil—a lot of people are watching," Derry tried to tell me.

"Let him go!" said Teresa. "Let him go, please. Please."

"Aw fuck," I said. "Why? Why him and not me? Because he's one of your lot, that's why, isn't it?"

Teresa just started bawling her eyes out.

"Fucking Taigs," I said and let Seamus go.

"I'm going to fucking kill you," Seamus gasped, bent double. "My brother's in the Provos. When we get home I'm going to get him to blow your kneecaps off."

"Was that a death threat, Seamus?" I said.

Seeing men in the queue were going to intervene for the sake of Fatherly law and order, Derry dragged me away. "Time to go, Wil," he said.

I yelled back at Seamus: "Don't ever threaten unless you can back it up."

I shook off Derry's grip and walked away of my own accord.

Somehow, with me just walking to get away from Teresa and Seamus I ended up in front of the big sign for the Demon—it was this pair of red snake eyes staring out from the black of the Void.

There was nothing to be scared of. I joined the queue.

Derry did too; he stood beside me in silence.

And when our alloted time came we rode the Demon into the Void, the howling underworld beneath Great America.

THREE

Nothing.

I remember nothing of the journey back from the park. I have only one impression to offer: for me the yellow bus and all those Projectees in it were not perched precariously on a single stack above the Void. They had fallen in. Or rather, Freddy had sucked them in.

Nada.

I did nothing the next day. I refused to get up in the morning. I refused to have the curtains opened. And no matter what Derry said or did I would not have a bite to eat, I would not break my fast. Hunger strike! If it was a good enough form of protest for Body, I mean Bobby Sands, and those other Taigs it was good enough for me.

Zippo.

I felt nothing when Mom Horrowitz came into the bedroom around noon to sweet-talk me and feed me milk and chocolate-chip cookies.

"What's wrong?" she said.

I wouldn't say.

"Is it this girl?" she said.

Silence.

"Derry said you liked her, right?"

Silence.

"She's not the only one. There are plenty more girls in the world, you'll see. When you grow up they'll all be running after you."

I used silence as my defense.

"Why don't you and Derry go out and do something? Wouldn't that be fun?"

Defense.

She went to the window. She ripped open the curtains. "You can't stay in bed all day moping. It's not good for you!"

Defiance.

"Get up!"

Passive resistance.

She came over and pulled me out of bed. I was naked when the covers fell away. Embarrassed, she wrapped a blanket around me. "Now come on, Wil," she said. "You're not staying in here a moment longer!"

Diddly-squat.

She could take me out of the bedroom and sit me down in the TV room, but there was nothing she could do to make me come back. I sat there with a blank look on my face, and a blanket around my body. Yeah, that's how I sat the whole of that Saturday.

Mom Horrowitz kept laying food in front of me and making me iced teas, none of which I laid a hand on.

"He isn't eating. Do something!" I heard her tell Derry in the kitchen.

"What?"

"Anything!"

"Just leave him alone Mom. If I know Wil he'll snap out of it when he's ready."

But she wasn't to be told. "I said, do something and I mean it!"

Nothing.

Derry took me outside, into that garage full of American antiques, and tried to show me how to refit Suzi's engine, but he could see I was far far away so he gave up trying and did nothing.

That is, until my own dirty protest against the Project and the hated Them. The Them that had brought me this low. All those fucking dirty Taigs! Aye, I thought—Fuck you, Seamus! Fuck you, Teresa! Fuck you, Peter! Fuck you, Counsellor Ciaran! And fuck the Pope and the IRA most of all!

I protested against them all by voiding myself; yeah, I pissed myself; I pissed myself and shat out a snakey turd that coiled around my calf.

"Aw Jesus, Wil," Derry said.

Then he did something that meant something, something that was not nothing, something tender, that made me want to come back for him, for us, for the Metal Mafia if nothing else. Without another word, he got some ol' rags and cleaned me up and then he mopped up the pool of piss. And the way he did it I knew he wouldn't ever tell. That's loyalty for you! Brotherhood unto death!

Thing is though, it's hard to come back from that far gone, and I couldn't quite make it.

When what people call the real world ceases to be, the inner world—as opposed to outer—comes into focus. When the ego—the instrument the Father fashioned in His own image for acceptable social intercourse—breaks up, the self, the true archetypal instinctual mind, is revealed. When dreams are no longer metaphors of the passing day but metaphysical realities of the eternal Void-night, we cannot help but see what is what for what it is. I say "we" because thanks to your man Wes Craven you'll probably have had something like this nightmare too.

I was lying in bed that night lost in sleep when one, two, Freddy came for me. I could smell him in the room—he stank like you'd expect a rancid corpse fart to.

I sat up, tensed, all ready to fight for my life.

I heard his laughter mock me.

I stood up, in a boxing stance, and I called out for all I was worth, "He got out, Fonz, he got out of the cubicle!"

That's when the bed opened up beneath me like the mouth of hell.

I went in feet first.

Then it had me up to my knees.

Trying to get a grip on something, I grabbed ahold of my pillow. I clawed at the sheet on the mattress, but the hell-mouth swallowed me down.

Falling.

Falling.

I would fall until I hit rock bottom.

The Rev decided it wouldn't be right for me to go to church the next day in a blanket or anything else. The family left me in Derry's care and went to pray for my lovesick soul as the Rev put it.

When he was sure they'd gone, Derry, my brother unto death, went to work on me. He shot off upstairs to raid his secret stash of sonic devil worship and returned with a record.

"Now this," he said, putting it on, "will rock your world!"

And it did.

What was it?

The devil himself's *Holy Diver*, that's what.

Yeah, it was Derry that dived down into the Void for me, but it was Ronnie James Dio who he used to rock the part of me I knew as me back from the bottom.

Of course, Ronnie James Dio isn't the devil. He might like to think he is, and us angry young Metallers, we liked to make believe that too. That's half the fun of Heavy Metal after all. But no kidding, the devil is more than a Satanic fantasy. See, the Christian devil is phenomenologically real. He is the Winnebago Trickster transfigured. He is Loki, Bacchus, Dionysus, Prometheus. The fiery creative intelligence of the self, the very essence of the shaman, hidden within us all. He is the Rainbow Singer. And he is evil only if you apply nonexistent morality to his behavior.

The Rainbow Singer is the opposite of God only if you believe in God the Father, and the rebellion of the son, and the original sin of patricide, and the fall from group grace. In the same way that God is not dead, neither is the devil. But he fell a long long way down from heaven. You have to try really really hard to call him up from the primitive depths.

I was glad to come back from those depths then; I can't tell you how glad, but now I really wish Derry had left me down there.

See, rock bottom is the place where shamans travel to willingly to unmake themselves, to kill the Father in them and to be reborn free as sons of Mother Earth. There, they find their Fonz if he can be bothered to show up and save them. There, they leave all the childish things of the Father's ego behind. Whereas I, Judas Carson, when I was called back by the fake devil, all I had was a shattered ego and no self, nothing to cling to: all I knew how to be was an Ulster Freedom Fighter. One of them. A dyed-in-the-wool Daddy's Boy. In point of fact "God!" was the first sound I gasped when I got back.

"Wil," was the first word I heard when I got back for sure.

"Derry," was the second word I said.

At that moment, almost like it was fated to be, I can honestly say those three words meant everything to me. Father. Brother. Me. I believed being part of this unholy trinity meant love. Father. Brother. Son. Love. Who needed women when you could be so hopelessly in love with men and their man's world?

When Mom Horrowitz and Tiara arrived back they were surprised to see me up and about, stuffing a tuna-and-cucumber submarine into my gob. In fact, or rather, in faith, they thought it was nothing short of a miracle.

"Praise the Lord!" said Mom Horrowitz and hugged me around the waist.

She grabbed me so tight I spat some tuna down into her face. She forgave me though, right off.

Tiara said, "I want you to know I prayed for you, Wil, even though you're such a little Irish creep."

Mom Horrowitz didn't hear Tiara because she was too

busy saying "Hallelujah! Wait until Pops sees this risen Lazarus."

When Pops did see me later on in the TV room he was pretty darn impressed with his foretelling abilities (which of course he hadn't shared with anyone but God in case he was wrong).

"I knew it," the Rev said, pointing at the ceiling. "I knew Jesus would heal you."

I couldn't help thinking if he knew it, why didn't he take me to the church and let his congregation see it happen right before their very eyes?

"Yeah," the Rev said. "God is a wonder-worker and no mistake. How do you feel son?"

"Better," I said.

"Lovesickness is a terrible thing," the Rev pronounced.

I said, "Aye."

"But you're over her now," the Rev said.

"Who?" I said.

The Rev laughed. "Who indeed? Little Miss Nobody."

"Yeah."

There was a break in the conversation, a deliberate pause for the Rev to think.

"Wil," said the Rev, "I think to celebrate your return from the dead we should do something tomorrow."

I was quick to take my opportunity: "Like what—go to the range?"

The Rev said, "The range?"

"Yeah."

The Rev shrugged. "OK, sure, the range it is. You can even pretend you're firing bullets into that Little Miss Nobody—let off some steam like I do when Mom gets on my nerves."

The Rev was kidding around and thought he was hilarious but I didn't dare laugh because, see, with that last remark he was bang on target.

30   HOME, HOME ON THE RANGE

The Rev kept both his guns at the range so how he was justified in keeping them for home defense purposes under American law was beyond me. If a prowler or a rapist or a serial killer came to visit for real he'd have had to jump in his Gay-Team van and drive for fifteen minutes there and collect them and drive for fifteen minutes back and by the time he got back his family would have been ogled, or fucked up the arse, or even cut to bits.

Now, you already know the Rev drove everywhere like that's what was at stake if he didn't get there on time. His life. His family. His immortal soul. Whatever. Never mind the dog collar, he was a truly maniacal driver-from-hell and no mistake. And that Monday morning, taking me and Derry to the range was no different.

"You fucking pissant ditwad motherfucker asshole!" was what seemed to stream out of his mouth for the full fifteen minutes it took us to get to the range.

What a high holy roller model—it was just too much! It killed us, like before, and we joined in once more.

When the Rev got out of the van he returned to normal. Me and Derry, we found that bit harder, because as sons we hadn't had nearly so much practice at it. When we were walking across the car lot outside the range some woman in a hurry nearly ran us over.

"You fucking ditwad!" Derry yelled at her and gave her the bird.

She honked her horn at us.

I shouted at her. "Fuck off you pissant motherfucking whorebag!"

We were all for trashing her car but the Rev wasn't having any of it. "Boys. Boys. Less of the language OK! And get out of the road!"

We obeyed him and the woman got to drive away.

The Rev said, "You ever hear of the saying 'Do as I say not as I do?' "

We nodded. It was more than appropriate the way we saw it.

"Well you don't have to say as I say or do as I do," said the Rev. "At least not all the time. Yeah?"

...

That was the Rev's first big mistake that day.

What do I mean? I mean, it's one of those things a father like the Rev, a traditional, conservative patriarch, should never say. See it strips him of the Father's (God's) cloak of power, the aura of infallibility he assumed in your childhood and used to control you.

Think about it—if the Rev as the father figure admits the Father can be wrong and do wrong and then gives you a gun—basically it's like handing you, the son, a license to kill. It's like saying, You can be and do wrong too, son, as long as you do it the right way, my way!

Of course at fourteen, picking the Rev's handguns up from reception, under a sign saying GUN-FUN FOR ALL YOUR FAMILY, I wasn't thinking exactly that: just something along those lines.

Out on the range the Rev clipped a loaded mag into the Beretta 9-mil and handed me it. Derry looked on, as I got my obligatory guest coaching session.

"OK, Wil," said the Rev, "being as you've never shot a gun before we'll go right back to basics." He pointed at the safety. "That's the safety. On—the gun won't fire even if you pull the trigger. Off—the gun will fire if you pull the trigger and no matter who or what it's pointing at. Keep it on until you have to fire. Yeah?"

"Yeah."

The Rev pointed at the magazine. "Pull that out."

I did like he said, only I went one or two steps further for Derry's benefit—I flicked out the top bullet, put it in again and slapped the mag back in place.

"You sure you've never done this before?" the Rev said.

"I watch a lot of movies," I replied.

That killed Derry. "Hollywood has a lot to answer for!" he said behind us.

The Rev laughed, a nervous laugh. "OK. Right. What you need to do next is you point the gun at the target up the range and squeeze the trigger. Don't pull the trigger. Squeeze. Yeah?"

I did like he said, kind of—I got into a pro's firing position and took aim at the shadowman target up the range. "Like this?" I said innocently.

"Yeah? Just like that. Now take the safety off and fire at will."

I emptied the whole clip into the target.

"Fuck me," the Rev said.

Because every shot was a head shot or a body-T shot to put the man down among the dead men like I'd been taught by the UFF.

Derry cheered. "See that! He's a natural, Pops, a natural!"

The Rev just stood there in amazement. Then he looked at me kind of funny. Suspicious like. "You sure you've never shot a gun before, Wil?" he said.

"Nah," I replied. "Why, was that good shooting?"

"Yeah," the Rev said.

I clicked the safety back on. "Then it's probably down to having such a good teacher, isn't it?"

The Rev liked his flattery he did. "Yeah, maybe you're right," he said. "Yeah. Try it again."

So that's how I spent the entire morning, firing the Beretta, pretending to miss occasionally so the Rev would feel useful, until I knew all the quirks of that particular gun like the back of my hand.

While the Rev was away getting a soda (he said he didn't want to do any shooting) Derry came over to me. He was touting the .357 Smith & Wesson hand-cannon. "Are you thinking what I'm thinking?" he whispered to me.

"What's that exactly?" I whispered back.

"I keep seeing that fucker Seamus' face on my target," he said.

"Yeah?"

"Yeah."

I kept seeing Teresa's more than Seamus' but I wasn't going to tell him that. "So?"

Derry held his hand-cannon up and, with his eyes gleaming gamma-green, said, "So let's waste him. I mean, he threatened to kill you, Wil, to kneecap you."

"He did, didn't he?"

"It'd be self-defense."

"Yeah."

"Yeah!" the Hulk roared, kind of quietly mind you, so's not to draw too much attention.

Our plan to get the guns home was a simple one, and as always, the simpler the plan, the better it works. It relied on one thing—the impatience of fathers to be getting back to do their own things, things they were good at, and not hanging around with their sons, which they're bad at.

When the Rev came back with his cherry soda, I was watching Derry have a go with the hand-cannon. Derry was a pretty good shot, nearly as good as me, so I didn't have to fake the praise too much.

"You've taught him really well too, Pops," I said.

"Yeah," the Rev said.

"Aren't you going to have a go, not even one?" I said.

The Rev shrugged and said, "I've got a sore shoulder. I don't really feel up to it now."

I knew what he meant was he wasn't going to show himself up to be worse than us but I let him get away with saving his ego. "Well then, maybe we should get going, eh Derry? I mean it's not fair us just blasting away with your Pops sitting bored out of his mind on the side-lines, is it?"

"Nah," said Derry and did like he said he would. He looked at his gun and said, "But it'll take ages for us to clean the guns."

That's when the Rev made his second big mistake that day. "You can do it at home this week," he said, like Derry knew he would.

When we got back into the van I said to the Rev as sincerely as I could, "Thanks very much, Pops. I enjoyed that loads."

"Yeah," said Derry. "That was great!"

The Rev smiled, then he got back to yelling at other drivers—so much he didn't notice that our pockets were bulging full of ammo.

Back at the manse, me and Derry hid our stolen cache of ammo with his stash of sonic devil worship—under the floorboards in his upstairs room.

"Nice one," I said.

"Yeah," he said back.

When we went downstairs Tiara took great pleasure in telling me, "Your Pops phoned while you were out. He says he wants you to phone him back immediately you get in. He sounded real pissed at you."

I got the Rev's permission to phone home and, to keep up appearances, did like I'd been told. I knew it was about my Ma and I was in for a right bollocking though.

The phone rang for ages and all that while I thought if I could just get away with not talking to him . . . But then he answered, "Wil, that you?"

"Hi, Da."

"Aye right," Da said his voice tin-thin on the phone. "What do you think you're playing at, son?"

"What do you mean, Da?"

"You haven't phoned your Ma in two bloody weeks!"

I tried to be conciliatory at first: "I know, I know, and I'm sorry, Da."

"Well sorry's not good enough. The woman's out of her

mind with worry, and hurt. If you were here I'd tan your hide for you I can tell you."

Tan my hide! No way. No way was he ever going to lay a finger on me, or even threaten to, again. That was it! "It's a crying shame I'm not there then," I said.

"What?"

"You heard me."

"What did you just say to me? What did you just say to me, you wee fucker!"

There was nothing else for it so I talked over the top of his ranting. "Listen, if Ma wants to give me grief you tell her to phone me herself. I don't want to hear it from you anymore, all right!"

That's when I put the phone down on him.

Da phoned back right after that, so's he could have the last word but when Derry got it, I just said to him, "Tell him to go and fuck himself!"

So that's exactly what Derry did. But he ad-libbed a few whispered swear-extras for good measure like ditwad and motherfucker and child-beater.

I think, against all odds, my Da must have gotten the message—that was the last I ever heard from him personally.

Derry took the phone off the hook, and kept it that way the rest of the day.

31 | HEAD-BANGED PRESS-GANGED

Me and Derry had to go to the Project group photo session whether we liked it or not. And we didn't! The pro-Taig Project was the enemy! But we couldn't say that. So we were going. That was Mom Horrowitz's word on the matter.

"But Mom?" I said.

"No buts, Wil!" Mom was not to be shifted.

It was a doomed protest, trying to get the matriarch to change her mind in her own kitchen, but it had to be made. I couldn't tell her that both Derry and me were worried that either Seamus or Teresa would have squealed on me and my Alien ball-busting; or that potentially there could be another fight; but I could make her feel as bloody guilty as I could about taking us.

"We were hoping to go to Summerfest!" I said. Summerfest was this big wingding downtown that Derry had been telling me about. You could watch live bands, pig out, you know?

"You can't miss the photo," Mom said. "And besides Stacey-May expects you there to do that article."

"Christ and a night!" I said.

"No blasphemy in this house, Wil!" Mom yelled. "How many times do you need to be told?"

What made things worse was that we had to get our photo taken in our hopeless rainbow T-shirts.

"This is getting to be like wearing a uniform," I told Derry in the bedroom as we were getting ready.

"Yeah," he said back.

"Let's do something with them, you know like?"

"Lose them?"

"Yeah," I said. "And what if we wear some old Metal T-shirts beneath them and put them on when we get rid of the others?"

"Cool," he said. "But the only Metal T-shirts Mom hasn't thrown out are my KISS ones and I've kept them unwashed under the floor for nearly a year. They probably stink."

That's how we turned up at the Methodist church hall for the photograph. Looking the part like every other little Projectee. But most definitely not being it underneath, or smelling like it either.

When Mom Horrowitz had dropped us off in the car lot

we snuck off into the bushes, took off the hopeless T-shirts, and left them in there. Thinking we'd been very clever we walked away from the bushes up to the bank upon which everyone was being gathered together for the photo.

When Counsellor Ciaran saw us in our black KISS T-shirts he was as horrified as we could have wished for. "What are you two playing at? Weren't you told to wear your rainbow T-shirts for the photo?"

He marched us straight to Stacey-May.

Unfortunately, when she saw us she wasn't horrified. "I might have known it would be you deliberately forgetting this year, Problem Child. Here, take this."

She handed me a new glowing-white rainbow T-shirt.

I looked at the size: XL. "It's the wrong size," I said, thinking that would get me off wearing it.

"Beggars can't be choosers," was all Stacey-May had to say on the matter.

When I put the darn thing on it drowned me. The one she gave Derry was huge too. I'm convinced they were ones she'd had personally made for her XLard-arse self.

"Now get in line, people," Stacey-May said as the photographer set up his camera. "I want the little people at the front and the big people at the back."

I wasn't going to be one of the little people—I was no Taigy leprechaun—so I went up the bank to the back of the crowd with Derry. Unfortunately, all boys big or small, Prod or Taig, Scots, Irish or American, like to be thought of as big, so that's where Seamus and Peter and Merrick and Joe were standing too.

"What are you doing back here, Carson, you dwarf?" said Seamus.

"Fuck away off and die," I told him.

"You fuck off you fucking Proddy dwarf!" said Peter.

Things were in danger of escalating prematurely into something so, to jeers and leering cries, me and Derry swallowed our pride and walked down the bank to the front.

All things in good time.

As soon as everyone was in line, Stacey-May shouted out, "Cheese!" and hey presto, the photo was taken.

Wouldn't you know though, the photographer said someone up the back had gone and spoiled it by sticking their fingers up behind someone else's head (Peter or Seamus no doubt). We did it again and someone else had pulled an ugabug face (Big Michael likely). Again and someone else had been hoking at their nose (I'd lay money it was Helmut). And again—two halions raised their right hands in the Metal 666 salute (that was us, Kids In Satan's Service, the Metal Mafia).

We had to do one more cheese before the group torture was finally over!

My own torture however, was to go on.

I don't think Stacey-May ever moved so quick in her life as when she came over at the end of the shoot to take my hand and have me off to the side for her interview.

"How long's this going to take?" asked Derry.

"Not long," she told him. "Run along and play with yourself somewhere."

I saw Derry scowl at her, but I wasn't going anywhere—except where Stacey-May wanted me to.

"Why do you want me to do this interview, Stacey-May?" I said.

"Maybe it's because you aren't like all the rest," she said.

"What do you mean?"

She was looking out to nab the somebody else she had in mind for the interview. "Where's she gone?"

"What do you mean?"

"This lot were all selected from the middle class for their leadership abilities."

"They were?"

"Uh-huh."

"And you don't think I was?"

"I know you weren't," she said smiling down at me. "That's what makes me interested in what you have to say."

"That's great, that is," I said all insulted.

"What's the smell?" she said. "That you?"

"Nah. It's my KISS T-shirt."

"Stinks."

I shrugged. "Yeah."

You'll never guess who Stacey-May collared for her other victim?

Yeah—the Taig-bitch from hell—skinhead Teresa!

I couldn't believe it!

But Teresa refused point-blank to do the interview. "Not with him," she said to Stacey-May, and walked away to join Seamus on the bank.

If I'd had the Beretta then . . .

Stacey-May wouldn't let Teresa get away so easily though. She called her back over and went to work on her. "Why won't you do the interview with Wil?" I overheard Stacey-May demand. "I thought you two were friends?"

"We were," I heard Teresa say, all sorrowful like. And the way her voice sounded aw, it almost broke my heart all over again.

"Then why?"

I could see Teresa was nearly in tears. "No reason."

"Good. So you agree to do the interview?"

"OK," said Teresa.

At that moment I felt sorry for her. Feeling returned in a rush. An uncertain tenderness. Followed by empathy. Then I remembered her kissing Seamus in front of me and I felt empty, like I was in the Void again.

"No way," I said to Stacey-May, pointing at Teresa.

"Yes way, Problem Child."

I folded my arms tight. "Nah, and you can't make me!"

"I have a noon deadline for Friday on this so you're it or else I'm going to have to tell Bishop Clement O'Riley about your second fight in Great America."

"You'd stoop to blackmail?" I said.

"Uh-huh. Works for me when nothing else does."

The clever bitch! She had me by the balls.

Needless to say the atmosphere was a little tense when me and Teresa had to sit down in the church hall and, under duress, talk about the Troubles with Ulster. We sort of represented them, see, in a metaphorical sense. We weren't speaking to each other or looking at each other or anything. And we were intent on winding each other up with our answers to political questions: well, I know I was.

Like when Stacey-May asked, "Do either of you think there is a solution in sight to Ulster's problems?" I answered right off the cuff, "Nah." But Teresa went and said, "Yes. I think that over time schemes like the Ulster Project will help to reduce the intolerance and bigotry and violence among the two communities."

And like when Stacey-May asked, "Have you made friends with people from the other side on the Project?" I answered, "Yeah, but then they showed their true colors. Green. White. And gold." But Teresa said, "Yes. I've made some good Protestant friends on the project and I look forward to keeping up those friendships when we return home."

The politically correct line of questioning went on like that until Stacey-May did the dirty—she pulled out her camera and asked us: "When are you two going to make friends again?"

That took me completely by surprise.

I shot a look at Teresa—

Who was looking at me too—

For a split second, lit up by the lightning flash of Stacey-May's camera, we stared into each other's eyes. I looked deep into those soul-windows, but I couldn't find what I'd seen in there before. It had already been had away by that thieving Taig Seamus!

I walked away.

I wish now I'd stayed and talked some, but I walked away.

That night I had another American Dream gone wrong.

I was back at the swimming pool, back at the pool party where I'd kissed Teresa and tasted the fire of Jack D. on her tongue. Only, I was alone in the pool and it was dark. Yeah, I was alone in the cold dark water when I saw something floating in the middle of the pool. It was a dark hump, looked like the coil of a Leviathan coming out of the deep or something. I swam over to see what it was, like stupid kids do in stupid horror movies, and when I got there I saw it was a body. I don't know why but I was compelled to turn it over, see who it was.

You know who it was?

That's right.

The Fonz.

You know what that means, don't you?

Yeah, my mentor was dead, my superego gone. Murdered by the looks of it. The Fonz's back was shredded by slash marks, marks that could only fit the glove of Freddy.

33 | SUMMERFEST

I'll be honest. I didn't much care if the Fonz was dead back then. When I woke up I thought, so what? Good riddance, he was a small Italian Taig and he didn't give good advice. In fact, he made a fool outta me, a love Judas. So the fuck what? It didn't matter. None of it mattered, except maybe going to Summerfest! I was up for that all right. A festival of eating, and drinking. And being merry with Derry.

So that's where we went that last Wednesday of my freedom. At two in the afternoon Mom Horrowitz took us downtown, to beside the Great Lake, where festival tents sprawled over the acres of a predevelopment waterfront site.

She dropped us at the pickup point for cabs.

"I'll see you back here at ten," she told us.

"Eleven, Mom, please?" pleaded Derry. "Or we won't see this INXS band."

"Ten-thirty."

"Eleven."

Mom tutted. "Ten-thirty. Take it or walk home."

"OK," said Derry, tutting back at her. If only he'd known how we'd regret not getting an earlier lift.

We had to buy a special pass to get into all the gigs during the day and the big twenty-thousand-plus rock concert that evening. I think it was about twenty dollars' worth but I took my program and paid the man almost gladly. I still had a bunch of my Da's dollars to spend even if I wasn't talking to him ever again!

I looked about me. It was wall-to-wall people, clustered around the sound stages, the stalls, the tents, the burger bars, the beer bars, the pizzerias, the German restaurants. I mean, I'd never seen anything like it. With the number of people in one place, it almost scared me. To get out of the crush we went and got an ice-cold Coke from a drinks machine and mooched around some by a stall, all the while just looking.

"This comes here every year?" I said to Derry.

"Yeah," he said. "Don't you have something like it in Belfast?"

"Nah. They don't do anything. No bands want to come to Northern Ireland. Except those Taigs U2."

"They're Taigs?" asked Derry, sounding well surprised.

"Aye of course they are. Did you ever hear that song 'Bloody Sunday'?"

"Yeah," he said.

"That's a Provo song."

"I don't believe it," he said. "I bought that *War* album!"

"Well," I told him, "now you know you most likely funded the IRA."

"Shite!"

We hadn't had much for lunch. Just a few ham rolls. So pizza was a number one priority. We stopped at this Little Italy Pizzeria. They were giving out all different kind of pizza samples for next to nothing. We took about four pieces each, sat down, gorbed, and watched the world go by.

"How many people get shot dead in Ulster every year, Wil?" Derry said with a mouth full of stringy mozzarella.

"Fifty or so. Maybe a hundred if it's a bad year."

"No shit! Way more people get murdered in Milwaukee every year than that!"

"That right?" I said.

"Yeah!"

We sampled some folded-over pizza then Derry got to speaking his mind again. "I thought it'd be a lot more."

"Nah. It flares up and dies down, you know?"

"That's because they don't do it right, do they? They just retaliate."

"Who?"

"Your lot—the Prods."

"Why—what do you think we should do?"

"You should just kill all the Taigs like Hitler did with the Jews, yeah?"

"Aye. Maybe you're right."

Derry burped. "Pizza's good isn't it?"

I burped back, "Yeah."

When we'd quite finished decibelching and discussing genocide, we went and watched what the program advertised as a Sawgrass Blues band. The music was good but it got me down, threatened to get me so down that I'd be among those dead men again. See it was all about losing your no-good baby to another man!

"Let's go," I said to Derry.

So we made our way through the crowds to the next stage up the walkway. Some Country and Western band were steel-guitaring away there and we didn't want to hear that guff so we moved on—or at least we tried to because that's when a shrill voice cried out from the crowd behind us:

"Psycho! Psycho Horrowitz! Is that you?"

Derry and me turned around and that's when I met the mutant with braces he'd boasted about snogging—you remember—the lovely Anne? Of course he didn't want me to put two and two together when we saw her, because she was this tall skinny thing with a mouth like your man Jaws out of *Moonraker*, and a face like the pizza we'd just eaten.

"Hiya, Psycho!" Anne said.

"Oh no," Derry replied.

"Long time no see!"

"Yeah," Derry said.

"Killed anybody lately, Psycho?"

Derry scowled at her.

Anne wasn't put off. "Well, aren't you going to introduce me to your little friend?"

"This is Wil," Derry said. "Wil, this is—"

It was clear he didn't want to finish that sentence—ever—so Anne butted in. "Hi, Wil," she said with a big metal smile. "I'm Anne, Anne Anderson. I used to go to the same high school as Psycho here."

"Hi there," I said, trying hard not to snigger at the thought of Derry and her french-kissing in the radioactive mutant USA.

She cottoned onto my accent: "You're foreign?"

"Aye."

"I know—you're Irish," she said.

"He is not Irish!" Derry told her before I needed to.

"You're Scottish then?"

"He's not that either," Derry said.

"Where are you from?"

"Never mind," I said. "It doesn't matter."

"Northern Ireland," Derry told her like he meant to scare her away.

"Oh there!" Anne exclaimed. "So what are you guys doing here—you going to plant a bomb or something?"

"Yeah," Derry said.

I could hear the Hulk in his voice so I had to act. "We've got stuff to talk about, Anne," I said, smiling all the while. "Be a good girl and fuck off."

She wasn't used to being talked to like that! You want to have seen her jaw drop open—I swear I've never seen so much heavy metal in my life!

We walked away. I was definitely getting good at walking away on women.

I thought it best not to rip the pish about Anne. We did have serious stuff to talk about. What was it? You already know in your heart of hearts the stuff we had to talk about was the where and the when and the who we were going to hit. You already know I'd done this sort of thing a hundred times with Alco and the Hit Squad. And yeah, I knew the operational rigmarole down to a tee but somehow, things seemed more strained, more difficult. The reason: for me anyway, it was because we were talking about premeditated killing. The sort that gets you charged with Murder One by the American Justice System.

Even if it's a so-called "Political Crime."

Even if you're fourteen.

Even if you were brought up from day one to hate Taigs so much you could kill them (though that's the real crime).

We made our plans overlooking the Great Lake, supping up our black coffees. They say coffee gives you short-term amnesia.

Maybe that explains Derry's misinterpretation of what

we, the last of the criminal brothers, were aiming to do in Round Six? I don't think so myself. How come I remembered then? I downed two plastic cups to his one, and I still managed to hold onto the idea that this was war, not murder.

"It's got to be at the leaving party," Derry said. "That's the last day, when the Taigs'll all be together in one place."

"Yeah," I agreed.

"We'll take Suzi, ride over there and let them have it!"

What with Derry's gung-ho attitude it was like being home again, talking to Rick the Prick or Brian or Wee Sammy. I couldn't help being the cautious one.

"We'll have to get some balaclavas," I said.

"What are they?"

"You know—terrorist head-gear? Like a black woolen hat with eyeholes and a mouthhole."

Derry looked blank.

"You must have a military surplus store in Milwaukee?" I asked him.

Again Derry looked blank.

"We need them so we don't get recognized, yeah?" I said.

Derry was miles away, staring out over the lake. "OK?"

"And we need combats. Clothes that we can throw away."

"OK?"

"And maps of the area for the getaway."

"Whatever," Derry sighed. "The big stage ought to be on now. Let's go laugh at Kool and the Gang!"

So that's what we did. We went and sat on these empty bum-numbing wooden benches right at the back of the arena and waited for Kool to appear.

When the Gang came onto the stage there was hardly anyone in the place—must have been a thousand, tops—and they were all up at the front ready to boogie.

The Gang warmed up for a brave while and then when they'd got it together, they started to play the one Kool and the Gang song everybody knew: "Celebration." And at the right moment Kool the boogie man came on in this pink sequin outfit and started shricking for everybody-everybody to celebrate good times.

That killed us that did.

We'd had well enough by song two and left about halfway through, but even outside the arena, at around five-thirty, we heard the concert end with another tired rendition of "Celebration."

Derry laughed and raised his plastic Coke glass. "Celebrate good times, Wil."

I knocked his cup. "Aye."

"I'll take Peter," he said. "Seamus is all yours unless you want some help."

"Nah," I said. "I'll deal with him."

"Sure you will," said Derry. "You want another hot dog?"

We'd had four in a row already so I said, "Nah."

"You looking forward to INXS?"

"Yeah," I said. I hadn't heard any of their stuff but it was a live rock concert—something I'd never been to before.

Derry looked at me. "Bet you wish it was Van Halen though, don't you?"

"Yeah," I said. That was one of my dearest wishes never ever to come true all right. When I think about it—none of my dear American wishes came true in the truest sense of true. But then, they weren't really mine at all; they were just more fantasies on loan from the group mind.

We went and sat on those bum-numbing benches again to wait for INXS to come on. The program said they were due to come on stage at eight-thirty.

We sat there for over an hour, with upward of ten thousand screaming fans watching and waiting for that band. They never did show though. See, another one of those lightning storms blew in across the Great Lake around eight. It started raining and it kept chucking it down the whole night. INXS at Summerfest was a total washout.

Derry and me were left there, taking shelter in a German restaurant, as the waters rose around us and night fell. That is, until the owner of the place kicked us out for taking up his space and not eating his food.

We went and stood under a tent near the entrance.

When we were just about the last ones still on site at nine, it dawned on me we had an hour and a half more to kill before we were collected. "Good this, isn't it?"

"Yeah," said Derry sarcastically.

About half an hour passed in pissed-off silence and teeming
rain. I was cold and wet and I wanted to talk about something so I said, "You know that girl Anne?"

"Yeah," he said.

"Did you really snog her?"

Derry was a little too emphatic with his, "Yeah!"

"Honestly?"

He shook his wet head. "Nah. I was going to ask her out
but—"

"She kept calling you Psycho?"

"Something like that."

That's when I got to thinking maybe I was lucky to have
kissed Teresa, snogged her in her bikini? What do they
say—yeah, it's better to have loved and lost than never to
have loved at all? Maybe it is, I thought. Even if your love
was for a Taig who betrayed it?

Derry must have read my thoughts—or my face—or
something because he said, "How are you going to do her?"

"Who?"

"Teresa," he said.

The rain came down. I had no answer.

"Are you going to kill the Fenian bitch right off or make
her suffer?"

I had no answer.

"You should make her suffer—shoot her through the
hands and feet—give her stigmata like Jesus, you know?"

I made no answer.

"You are going to kill her, Wil, aren't you?"

Under duress I said, "Yeah."

"Well you better start thinking about how you're going to do it then, hadn't you?"

The rain came down.

By ten-thirty when Mom Horrowitz collected the drenched pair of us, I regret to say I had the notion of how I would do it. I would shoot Teresa once through the heart.

Everybody knows Hollywood Horror is all about how many sequels you can milk from one scary story. It's the same with bad dreams: once the director, aka the self, gets cracking they just run and rerun and run.

I found myself to be an Oakland Raider, standing with my four shadows surrounding me (due to floodlighting) on the pitch in the Green Bay Stadium. I was playing in front of a packed house, baying for blood; still I could hear the commentator announce over the tannoy: fourth down at the forty-yard line.

666. 666. 666. Hut-hut-hut. That was my cue to run. I ran. See, somehow, I knew I was a wide receiver supposed to

be running for a pass, across the thirty, the twenty. I was running full pelt looking for the spiral; looking for that spiral to complete the pattern play. The ten. The five. End zone coming up, ball spiraling in. Catch. Touchdown in sight . . .

Wham!

I got hit.

The Beast of Green Bay took me down, trounced me.

And while I was on the ground he started to pull his yellow trousers down.

I couldn't defend myself because I couldn't move. I was winded. My ribs felt like they were all broken. I looked over to the sidelines for help. Derry? But he wasn't there. Instead, I saw one of the Raiders cheerleaders—a bald one with a bleeding heart . . .

—Teresa? cheering the Beast on. And my coach, my coach who was Freddy, was jumping up and down shouting, "Do it! Do him up the arse, Beast!"

The Beast ripped my silver trousers down and pulled my jock to the side.

DREAM OVER

When I woke up it was morning. I was panting with panic. The sheets were drenched with sweat. And my head felt really, really heavy and fuzzy . . .

It was only then I noticed the bars running horizontally across my face.

Was I in prison?

Nah. That was when it struck me, freaked me out—I was wearing a football helmet. And I could guess whose too.

I leapt up out of bed and I yanked the helmet off me. When I saw it was a beat-up yellow with a green and white G on it I knew.

The number 666 confirmed it.

But that was OK. See, I knew the arse-bandit Beast was a dream, wasn't it?

DREAM OVER!

When I woke up it was still night, darkest night. I was lying with no clothes on me, not even a sheet.

I wiped the beads of sweat off my brow. I sighed. The football nightmare was over. The Beast. Freddy. Teresa. It was just a stupid dream.

I looked over at Derry who was still fast asleep. I envied him his peace. Why didn't he ever have nightmares? Then I thought—if he was awake right now, he'd see me naked, so I reached down to the side of the bed to pull up my sheets.

That's when I noticed it.

I was fat. Potbellied fat like my Da, like I was pregnant with another son, a better son, a son of the Beast and a son of Belfast.

That's when I felt it—the life inside me—kick to get outside of me. I went into labor. Male labor. Which isn't the same as female labor because there was nowhere and no way for this fetus to get out, come out, except to rip its way out—

Like an Alien.

And so I became one of those doomed Daddy-boy Marines, hanging up on the walls of that failed terraforming colony, birthing my own Alien. Like they did—I screamed and I screamed as I saw the head chew its way out of my guts . . .

DREAM OVER?

When I woke up it was early morning, around seven. I
was sweating. I was panting. I didn't know what way was
up, what way was down. All-told, I was a fucking mess.

"Derry!" I called out.

"Yeah," he answered me back, groggy-voiced.

In relief—that it wasn't a dream—I said, "Nothing."

Derry fell silent, back to sleep, again.

Feeling a lot like the poor haunted Johnny Depp in the
original *Nightmare,* I did not dare close my eyes. Just in case
I dreamt . . .

My fear was the fear of the unknown, of the nothing to be
scared of, the Void. I was a living Father Freddy's own
dream. I hadn't a baldy about the meaning of things, the
meaning of life, what my American dreams and nightmares
meant, if anything. Like I say, they just scared the crap out
of me, made me think I was losing my mind.

Now though, it's a different matter, at least I think it is.
See, I've read up on it while doing my hard time in Isolation
(what else is there to do except wank?). If Jung's to be
believed—and I'd take Jung's dream theory over Freud's
any day of the week—what I experienced was the start of
the process of individuation.

Yeah, like Jung says, my unconscious had been activated
by a wounding. My unconscious, mind, not the collective
unconscious, not the group mind, or the Father's ego. Mine!

And once all that happened, I had to pass through my own shadow—the unconscious as symbolized by Freddy and the dream-Beast—to get to the center of my persona— the self (aka the genius inside us all). The center of my self was an Alien to me, metaphorically speaking, hence my rape-child: the first fetal stage of the Alien.

If only I had dared to close my eyes, to dream, to dare to dream my own Alien dreams like Ridley Scott, I would probably have woken up to what life is, found more of myself, and wouldn't have fought back so violently against my own shadow.

But—

I was a Loyalist caught up in the Father's own dream. How was I to know? Nobody tells you these things. Certainly not your father—unless he is not a representative of the Father at all but a shaman, who has vision-quested to the Void and sung up the primal rainbow. The red and yellow and blue, of his own lost self.

So there you have it. Freddy. The Beast. Aliens. It was beyond me. And I was well trained by the narrowing minds of Ulster that things that were beyond me didn't bear thinking about. Yeah, instead of thinking about saving my self, I figured I should think about what I could do for others, what I could do for my country. I remembered Alco's ol' sayings: "There's too many Taigs in the world." "The only good Taig is a dead Taig." "It's us or them so it's them, son!"

I decided I didn't want to go back—to sleep, to dream—

ever. I would live in "the real world," the world my Father dreamed up. It may not have made much sense but it made more sense than nothing. So, I got up, got Derry up, and got on with the day. There was a lot to do. A lot to take my mind off my self.

First things first, we had a quickie breakfast of Rice Krispies. And while the bowl snapped, crackled and popped I set about locating an army surplus store in the local directory. I found one in New Berlin.

"You know where Frederick Strasse is?" I asked Derry.

"Yeah. I think it's on the main bus route into town."

"Cool."

With the destination fixed, we were on our way. It was ten to eight—plenty of time to get there and back and get everything else done in the afternoon.

We'd just opened the front door when—

The Rev called us from upstairs: "Derry? Wil?"

We both said, "Yeah, Pops?"

"Where are you guys going?" the Rev said.

Derry fielded that one: "Wil wanted to do a bit of last-minute shopping in New Berlin before he went back?"

"At this time?"

"Yeah," I said. "It's for my Ma and Da."

"If you can wait an hour your Mom will take you in," the Rev said.

I was firm. "No, Pops. We're going to get the bus, OK?"

The Rev couldn't believe it. "The bus? Are you sure you'll be able to recognize a bus if you see one, Derry?"

That sort of patronizing patriarchal question was insulting to sons everywhere so I backed Derry up—and we both answered, "Yeah!"

What else could the Rev say?

We left.

We got the eight-ten A.M. bus at the end of the road. We paid and sat down at the empty back seat of the bus. It felt good to be going somewhere without being lifted and laid. Adventurous like, you know?

A few minutes into the journey I saw a wild deer skitter across the asphalt into a suburban field.

I pointed and said, "Look!"

But Derry was looking the other way and missed it.

I was dead chuffed at seeing my first deer. "I didn't know you'd have deer around here?"

"Yeah, yeah," Derry said. "Me and this guy who used to go to school with me shot one up in the woods not far from here."

"You didn't?"

"Yeah we did. But it didn't die and it ran away. We couldn't find it to put it out of its misery."

"That's too bad," I said. "You know, I don't know if I could shoot a deer?"

"You could too—if it was a Taig deer!" he said, mimicking my accent perfectly.

Now that killed me stone dead!

. . .

Nobody's perfect: we got off the bus at the wrong stop on
Frederick Strasse. But we walked up it and sure enough—
there was the U.S. Army surplus store.

It was just opening up for the day when we tried to get in.
I say tried, because our way was blocked by this big red-
necked lummox in ex-Marine combats, lugging bargain-
basement stuff out into the street.

"Howdy." He scowled as he went by.

"Hi," we said back.

"You young guns are up bright and early," he said.

I read his name badge: it said Earl. Then I said, "Yeah.
We need supplies, Earl."

Earl dropped what he was doing. He stood up and wiped
his brow with a massive tattooed forearm. "That's a new
accent on me—where you from, son?"

"Northern Ireland," I told him.

Earl slapped his thigh. "No shit—you know your war then!"

"I do."

"He does," seconded Derry.

Earl held out his hand.

I took it and shook it. To my eternal surprise Earl didn't
try and crush my knuckles: he respected my grip strength,
or tolerated my grip weakness more like.

"What's on your mind, warrior?" Earl said as he released me.

"Combats," I said.

"And bala-things," Derry added, trying to sound like he
knew what he was doing.

Earl shot a look at Derry like he was an antiwar demonstrator or something. To me he said, "I got loads of ex–Vietnam Marine combats—some still have the bloodstains on them."

Now, I have to say the way Earl evil-eyed me as he said it, I knew not to respond. But Derry, he just went ahead and said, "Cool!"

Earl was not impressed. "Son, men fought and died for Uncle Sam in these uniforms. Show some respect!"

I pushed Derry in the direction of the combats.

"Let me do the talking in here, OK?" I told him.

"I just—"

"We don't want to be noticed any more than you have to be, all right?"

"I—"

"Put a cork in it, will you?"

Derry went into a sulk so I shopped for the both of us. I got two sets of combat fatigues—mine were of course too damned big, but I couldn't for the life of me find the balaclavas we needed.

"You got any balaclavas?" I shouted over to Earl.

"Top shelf at the back, son," Earl yelled back like a drill instructor.

I searched and found them.

I tried mine on. "What do you think?" I asked Derry.

"You look a bit like your masked man Jason out of *Friday the Thirteenth*," he said.

"Yeah? Put yours on—see if it fits?"

Derry did as he was told.

"Right," I said. "Let's pay the man."

When we got up to the counter, I handed over the goods.

Earl packed them up. "What sort of covert operation have you got planned, son—search and destroy, ambush?" Earl asked, having a military ha-ha-ha-ho laugh at us.

"Aw nothing like that," I said and laughed. "Just playing soldiers, Earl."

"Play Marines, son," Earl said. "We have better fun and we win more than the Army."

I copied Earl's laugh: ha-ha-ha-ho.

Derry did too.

I don't think Earl realized we were ripping the pish or if he did—he didn't want to lose his first sale of the day.

"That'll be thirty-nine dollars, Marine," said Earl and saluted me.

I forked out what was left of my Da's money while Derry took the bag of stuff.

Earl gave me the change back. "Keep your heads down, boys," he advised, "or you'll get them shot the hell off!"

It was good advice.

Derry should have heeded it but wouldn't you know, he was still too busy sulking.

The journey back by bus took a while but we got to the manse around ten-thirty.

There were no cars in the drive or on the lot. As always, the Rev must have been out ministering and Mom Horrowitz must have been out collecting that antique firewood of hers. But just in case Tiara was home and not shopping, I told Derry, "Drop that bag off in the fields out back—and remember where you put it."

When we got inside the manse, we crept into the kitchen.

"What about Tiara?" I said.

"Anybody home?" Derry yelled.

No reply.

So I asked Derry, "Where does Pops keep his maps?"

Derry shrugged, "In his van?"

"Where else? We have to look at those maps," I told him.

"I'll check his room," said Derry and ran upstairs.

Luckily enough it wasn't long before he hoked out exactly what I was looking for: a map of Milwaukee, our Happy Hunting Ground.

I spread the map out on the table.

"Where's that list of Projectees' addresses gone?" I asked Derry.

"It was by the phone," he said and went looking for it.

He found it on the kitchen table.

"What's Merrick Stulz's address?" I asked.

Derry looked it up. "Forty-five Lakeshore Drive, Muskego."

I found it in the street index and then pinpointed it by a small lake on the map.

Needless to say, we learned our route to and from the target several different ways, and we learned them all off by heart just in case we ran into trouble.

The next thing on the agenda was cleaning the guns. We were jumpy even at the thought of getting caught doing that even though the Rev had said it was Derry's job . . . Unfortunately, that was when the phone rang.

Derry jumped.

"Don't answer it," I said. "It could be my Ma."

That was when Tiara, complete with a severe case of bedhead, but only half-covered by her gray-white robe, rushed into the room.

"Oh, you're back!" she said.

The split in the front of the robe revealed her beaver. It was black, and bushy, and frankly, like the guys in *Porky's*, I couldn't take my eyes off it.

"What do you think you're looking at, Wil?" said Tiara, all stroppy like.

"Your beaver," said Derry.

"You little shits!" she yelled and pulled the robe over herself. "You little perverts!"

We just stood there and laughed our heads off.

She snatched up the phone and all-polite, said, "Hello?"

We were still laughing, when I heard Tiara say, "Yes I'll get your pervert of a son for you, Mrs. Carson."

I stopped laughing.

Tiara threw the phone at me. It was her turn to laugh.

I caught the phone. I had to speak to Ma, there was no choice but to take the bollocking in front of Derry and last-laughing Tiara. "Hi, Ma?"

"Wil. Who was that?" asked Ma, her voice shriller than tin-thin.

"Tiara," I said, giving Tiara the bird.

Tiara glared at me—a killer look.

"What does she mean 'pervert son'?" Ma asked.

"Nothing. She's just running around half-naked showing off that's all."

"Well I hope you're not looking—"

"Nah, Ma," I said. I was though. I watched Derry push Tiara out of the room, with her all the while slagging us off.

Derry came back to guard the doorway from his sister.

I heard Ma sigh. "Your father told me what you did to him."

"Did he now?" I said. "Good!"

"What?"

"I'm not taking anymore shite from him!"

"What!"

"You heard me."

"Now you listen here, young man—"

"Nah. You listen here Ma. When I come home I don't want to see Da again. He's done using me as his punchbag, all right!"

"Who do you think you're talking to, Wil? We're your parents! Put Mom Horrowitz on this instant till I tell her what to do with you."

"Nah, no way, Ma."

Derry came to my rescue again. He clicked the receiver down. "I would have pulled it out but that could get me grounded," he said. "And we need to be free, free to be we."

I was never as glad to get off the phone. "Ta, Derry," I said.

He took it off the hook again of course, so's Ma couldn't ring back like she would have.

What with Tiara running around we had to be more careful about things. I cleared the map off the kitchen table and folded it down into my pocket.

"Where are the guns?" I whispered to Derry.

"I'll get them," he said.

"Bring them to our room, eh?" I said, and went there myself.

Once Derry had got the guns from the Rev's study we went to work like a crack Marine unit. Stripping them down, cleaning every inch of them, inside and out. Putting them back where Derry had found them proved more difficult than the business of cleaning them—because Tiara stuck her nose in on the way.

"What's that you've got there, Wil?" she asked in the hall.

"Nothing," I said, holding a bundle full of cloth and Beretta.

But that wasn't good enough. She came to investigate. "I don't think it's nothing."

There was nothing else for it. Derry copped to it. "We just had to clean Pop's guns, that's all."

She was horrified. "I can't believe he brought them into the same house as the infamous Psycho, let alone allowed you to do that!"

"Don't call me Psycho," Derry told her.

"They're not loaded," I told Tiara, hoping the Hulk wasn't going to appear.

But thankfully Derry didn't have to get angry—Tiara took that as her cue to exit. She had the last words though—we allowed her that and they were good ones if I recall rightly: "Boys! Playing with their puds! Men! Playing with their guns! The world's all so goddamned phallic I can't take it anymore!"

We scurried away to put the guns back in the Rev's study where they would stay for one more day.

The biggest thing we had to do that day was fixing up Suzi our iron horse for the road trip across town to the target. It took hours of Derry's fiddling and fine-tuning to see her right from my crash.

While he was hard at that, I took some ingredients and made us both lunch—tuna and sweetcorn and mayo and cucumber subs. And then I took some other ingredients—petrol, washing-up liquid, and ripped-up bits of Stacey-May's jumbo rainbow T-shirts—mixed them in four bottles and bingo, we had Molotov cocktails for afters. Two each. I hid them down the field with our UFF uniforms.

Around four o'clock, Derry said of Suzi, "That's her done, I reckon!"

"You sure," I said back.

"Aye," he said and gunned the engine to life. "But we'll take her out for a spin just to be sure."

"Yeah OK—if you hop on the back."

"OK!" he said.

I took Suzi out for a test run. I raked the crap out of her

and she took it. Derry clung onto me, shrieking like a mad-man as I threw the bike into turns and through the mud.

We went around the circuit three whole times like that. At high speed, and I didn't make one mistake. It was great.

When I pulled up in front of the garage for the last time I said to him, "You can take her now."

But Derry replied, "Nah. I'll take her tomorrow. On the way there, at any rate."

For all the careful planning we did that day, the day before the killings, they were to label us, the Metal Mafia, mad. Like I said before—to them it wasn't a paramilitary opera-tion. To them it wasn't a political action. To them it wasn't a blow struck for the freedom of Ulster! To them it was incomprehensible that children would kill other children for the same reasons, the same Cause, as adults would kill adults.

In his summing-up the judge cited Derry as, get this—"a secret devil worshipper, and a suspected psychopath." And you'll laugh at this—he labeled me an "evil sociopathic child-killer." I have to tell you. That totally kills me! That judge. That father figure who sat there all swelled up, proud, fat, and ol', representing Uncle Sam's justice system (that pro-Father, pro-group institution set up to organize revenge against group-transgressing individual sons). That there judge. Telling me I was evil. It totally kills me—and it might have if Wisconsin wasn't one of only twelve states not to have the death penalty back then! I mean, that there emanation of the Tyrant Holdfast, how could he know the truth?—Because he would not see he was a psychopath himself, suffering under his own mad illusions. He refused to admit he had buried his experience of the Alien inside himself in a hash-mash of patriarchal beliefs because he was scared shitless of it. That day in court, their day—not my day in court, he denied that my only crime was dreaming the Father's dream of Ulster, the Father's dream of the world.

36 | VOID

Wouldn't you know they're releasing all the political prisoners from both sides—Loyalist and Republicans—back onto the streets of Ulster these days of ceasefire, but I'm never getting out of here. Out of this man-made Void. Ever. I was sentenced to one and a half centuries of imprisonment, without possibility of parole, for what I did aged fourteen.

My last day of freedom began at eight with the biggest pile of flapjacks and maple syrup the world has ever seen. And me and Derry gorbed them down like there was no tomorrow.

When we were finishing them off the phone rang. Mom Horrowitz got it before we could sabotage it: "Hi?"

We watched her as she took the call.

I was praying. Please God. Not my Da. And not my Ma.

"Hi there, Stacey-May. What can I do for you?"

I was relieved.

But Derry said "Stacey-May!" and looked at me panic-stricken.

The pair of us, we tried to hear what was being said—but Mom must have felt our eyes and ears zooming in on her. She turned her back on us and spoke in low tones.

We didn't have to wait long for Mom Horrowitz to relay the message she'd been given.

"You two!" she tutted at us as she put the phone down.

"What now?" said Derry. "We haven't done anything!"

"That was Stacey-May," she said, coming over all disappointed in us.

We said, "Uh-huh—"

"About the Going Home Party today—"

We prompted, "Yeah—"

"It's at Merrick Stulz's place and can't be rearranged—"

We said, "We know—"

"Well, under the circumstances, what with the fight with his guest and everything, Stacey-May said maybe you two shouldn't go."

I think she expected us to be gutted so I said, "That isn't fair!"

Derry joined in. "Yeah, we went and shook their hands and stuff!"

Mom was not impressed. "Stacey-May mentioned something about further goings-on at Great America."

"That was Seamus," I said. "And she knows that!"

With her hands on her hips, the matriarch stood in her kitchen and said, "So there is more to the story? I'll have to tell your father when he gets back later today."

How many threats can a son take?

I walked out of the room.

Derry followed.

We stayed in our room, sulking, or at least giving a damn good impression of sulking, until Mom Horrowitz drove off to shop at one of her antique markets.

Little did she know we were going to that party even if it killed us!

Little did we know that she had set Tiara to keep a beady eye on us, and that because of all the blow-job blackmail, Tiara had every intention of doing just that.

Now we had to be at the Going Home Party by twelve-thirty to do our pre-op recce. That meant leaving at ten-thirty—at the latest.

At ten we had everything ready to go. We were all dressed in our KISS T-shirts and shorts. We had the ammo but we didn't have the guns.

So, we snuck out of our room to fetch them from the Rev's study. We got in undetected all right but who should we meet on the way out? Who else but Tiara.

"What are you up to, you little creeps?" she said.

"Nothing," we both said, and held our hands up to show her this was the case.

"Then why do you look so guilty?"

"No reason," Derry said. "You just scared us. You're a very scary person."

"Mom told me to keep an eye on you two. I can see why." We walked away.

I could feel Tiara's eyes burning holes in my back—it was almost like she had X-ray vision and could see the guns or something?

With the guns all locked and loaded we were ready to get the hell off hallowed ground.

Derry went outside to the garage and started Suzi up.

Once I heard the engine I went to join him, sliding out the window, with both the guns stuffed down my pants.

I made it around to the back porch and thought I was home and dry, when Tiara appeared again.

"Going somewhere, Wil?" she said.

"Out for a ride," I said.

"What's in your pants, Wil?" She pointed down at my bulging shorts. That's when it struck her. "My God! Those are Pop's guns aren't they?"

There was nothing else for it but to do what I did. I drew the Beretta and aimed it at her head.

"Don't you dare, Wil," she said.

"Shut the fuck up, Tiara!" I told her. "Down on your knees now!"

She wouldn't do it.

"On your knees," I shouted. "Or I'll shoot you dead."

The reality of the situation got to her. She dropped to her knees.

"Hands behind your head!"

She obeyed, whimpering a little. "Oh my God! Oh my God!"

"Derry!" I yelled. "Derry!"

I don't know how he heard me over the noise of Suzi but he came riding round.

"What the fuck are you doing?" was the first thing he said to me, only he said it real calm like.

"I couldn't help it," I said. "She saw the guns and freaked."

Tiara started crying. "Derry, stop Wil doing this. I'm your sister for God's sake."

Derry looked down on her and just laughed.

I don't mind telling you that Derry's laughing, Tiara's gurning, and the thought of what this all meant, terrorized me. "Aw fuck! What are we going to do now?"

"We'll tie and gag her up," Derry said, taking command. "And then—put her down in the cellar."

It wasn't very big and it wasn't very clever and it wasn't to be very effective either, but that's exactly what we did.

When we came up from the cellar I was sweating it big-time. See, we'd come so far that even if we didn't go through with the op we were fragged, we were toast, we were Rancheros burgers. There was no way Tiara wasn't going to tell on us. None.

But Derry didn't seem fazed. He said to me, "Did you

honestly think we were going to get away with this, Wile E. Coyote?"

"Yeah!" I said.

"Well I always knew we weren't."

"Nice of you to tell me," I said. I was shaking.

"Do you still want to do it? Do you still want to strike a blow for God and Ulster against those dirty Taigs?"

Put like that, what with all I believed in back then, it was hard if not impossible to say no, so I said, "Aye, I do."

We went and got into our marine surplus (in my case surplus plus) uniforms, stuffed our balaclavas into our top pockets, and tucked the guns into our green belts. We must have looked a right sight as we mounted Suzie and rode away from the Horrowitz manse.

At the bottom of the road to home Derry and me turned for one last look and then we were off.

It was funny the way we were nearly caught ten minutes later.

Nah, not by the cops—we were keeping a close eye out for them.

By the Rev in his Gay-Team van.

We were raking up one of the unavoidable stretches of main road when over Derry's shoulder I spotted the Rev heading straight for us (but coming in the opposite direction). I was sure he was going to see us, recognize us, come after us, stop us, punish us. I shouted a warning to Derry, pointed up ahead, but even if Derry had taken evasive action, it wouldn't have made any difference, wouldn't have saved us. The only thing that did was the Rev's road rage. See some ditwad asshole motherfucker had cut up the Rev and he was too busy swearing and giving them the bird to notice us zip by him on Suzi.

That killed us.

We took to the byways rather than the highways after that to cut down the risks of being spotted by cops. We did hear sirens wail close by a couple of times but they weren't calling to us (yet that is—Tiara had got loose by this stage and phoned 911 but, as it emerged at the trial, the police response time was deadly slow that day).

I'll swear, the way we buzzed south across those suburbs without getting noticed, it was almost as if we had become invisible, or at least urban-camouflaged to the point of invisibility. I mean, we weren't of course—there were a few drivers on the way who honked their horns at us, and one who shook his fist and yelled something (probably not "I can see you, you teenage terrorists you!")—but nobody, nobody tried to stop us.

So, we got to the jumping-off point at one o'clock. It was this woody knoll that I'd picked out on the map because it overlooked Merrick Stulz's Da's plush lakeshore mansion.

We were late so we dismounted sharpish and went to recce the scene below. At a distance—and it was about two hundred or so yards—we could see the Going Home Party was in full swing. A lot of the Projectees were swimming in the blue water of the lake. Others were playing volleyball on the garden by the shore. But they were all teeny tiny people—you couldn't make out who was who, Prod from Taig, for the life of you.

"They're all over the place," said Derry.

"Yeah," I said. "But look, I told you—as soon as lunch is served they'll all be together in the one place."

I pointed at the smoke rising from the barbecue. We could see Stacey-May cooking up the meat—she was no tiny person even at that range.

Lunch was nearly served.

That pleased Derry no end.

Our cue to begin the attack was Stacey-May calling them all to the barbecue lunch. Once we heard her yell Derry and me pulled on our balaclavas and drew our guns.

He smiled at me through the black wool mask. "Let's do it!"

I said, "Yeah!"

We flitted through the dappled shadows of the wooded area; down, down an overgrown trail to the edge of the asphalt surface of Lakeshore Drive. Before we broke cover, Derry slowed to a dead-stop and turned on me.

He was shaking. I could see he was shaking like a leaf.

"Hit me, Wil," he said. "Hit me hard in the face!"

"What?" I said back.

"Hit me!"

It was then I twigged what he was doing. He was trying to get angry, trying to make me make him angry so the Hulk would appear and fear-flight would turn to fear-fight. So without saying a word, I hit him, I hit him hard in the mouth.

He winced on contact, staggered back a little.

"Are you all right?" I said.

He spat some foamy blood out onto the trail and glared up at me. In the balaclava slits his eyes glowed Hulk-green. "Yeah," he said. "That was just what the doctor ordered!"

The Hulk crossed the road at full pelt and ran twenty yards up the other side until he reached the driveway of the Stulz residence. I followed. I followed him past the pink Cadillac that I would never ride in, and all the way around the back.

At the last corner, the absolute point of no return, he stopped. He had a look around the corner. He looked back at me. He had another recce around it and looked back at me.

"Go. Do it!" I whispered.

The Hulk shook his head and said, "Remember, Wil— this is you defending yourself. You defending your country."

I told him straight. "I don't need a pep talk, Derry!"

"Yeah you do. Those two Taigs, Seamus and Teresa, are sitting out there laughing at you. They're laughing at you. Listen."

I listened and heard laughter.

"Do you hear? Every Taig on the Project is laughing at you, at us!"

I knew he was trying to wind me up. Trying to make me snap—like I had before with Seamus when the Alien ripped its way out of me. I remember thinking, I didn't need to be angry to do it, I needed to be cool. So I was going to be cool, not Kool and the Gang kool, but even cooler than the Fonz. Hey! Right?

Wrong. Instead, I turned into one of those damned Marines. I've spent a long time thinking why that happened. Reflecting. And I think I know why now. Yeah. I think it was Arthur Koestler who said that, because evolution is an add-on metamorphic process, man has not got one brain, but three: a lizard brain, a mammal brain and a human brain.

If you think about it this analogy is flawed, as was Koestler himself. What about the fish brain? Or the sea-worm brain?

But even if it is faulty, the idea can still be useful. See, this reptile brain could symbolize the most primitive part of the brain, the seat of all our human emotions and instincts. This Lizard, it would be like the Serpent in the Garden of Eden to man; man who is simply a group mammal with a massively overdeveloped Father-complex. It would rest within us. Waiting to burst out. To rip up what is left of the illusion of the conscious ego we have developed, and get back to raping and murdering basics.

This is where my Alien rips out into it.

Lizard—Alien. Alien—Lizard. Same thing in my book. And when you think about it, this fits too: Hulk—Lizard. Lizard—Hulk.

Fourteen- and fifteen-year-old Lizard-things. That's what Derry and me were when we did it. Not free-thinking individuals. Not Platonic moralists. But two group lizard-mammal-humans with massively overdeveloped Father-complexes acting out the dream of Us or Them self-defense.

The Hulk rounded the corner first. He didn't run. He walked in a kind of slow-mo—like it was a movie we were in—a Hollywood movie like *The Terminator*. He walked right up to where I saw Peter sitting joking with Seamus and Teresa.

Now, any terrorist worth his salt knows Terror takes time to spread, to take hold, because no one wants to believe bad things can happen to them and no one sees what they don't believe in. And so it was. Nobody seemed to notice us right off. All the Projectees were all too busy eating and drinking and having a laugh. Or maybe me and Derry were still blending into our environment, invisible like you know?

But then Derry raised his gun.

And fired.

Peter being blown away without a word; dead double-tapped in the head, without an Arnie one-liner to do it justice; that broke the Hollywood spell all right.

. . .

Now I know I'm dragging you away from the action by rattling on about this here but it needs saying. See, at the end of all this I don't want you to suffer the negation of experience, rather I want you to get an experience of negation. What do I mean? Well, it's like this. I'm worried you'll find my experience (especially the killing) to be disconfirming, constricting, discouraging, undermining of your own ego; that is, if you still believe in the Father's love. If you still believe in his love, like a good little Daddy's Boy or Girl, this will be the case. Love of the Father, love of the group, will negate your experience as an individual. Love will stop you experiencing the Void of my self for what it is. Love will not allow you to see what I have seen. All you will see is what fits what you have been brainwashed to believe. You will not see past the Ten Commandments and the due process of Law. Killing. Murder. Crime. Justice. Punishment.

The screaming was what I remember most about that terrific instant. The screaming of girls and more disturbing, that of boys. And then there was the roaring of Derry, the roaring of the Hulk gone berserk.

The world it seemed had gone mad.

But it hadn't—it was the same ol' world—the same ol' Metal soundtrack to the Father's wonderful world of love and violence and downright Terror.

Derry the Hulk was roaring at Peter's corpse: "That was for God and Ulster and the Metal Mafia!"

I had his back. And I had to cover his back—because all of a sudden Stacey-May was running at him, intent on tackling him, as intent on a sack as the Beast of Green Bay.

Now, you know I liked Stacey-May, I liked her a lot, but I also knew she was a woman who just wouldn't be told nah. I had Derry's back. There was only one option.

I shot her, twice in the chest.

The bullets knocked her away from Derry. She hit the ground hard and with a groan was still.

Nothing I can do will bring Stacey-May, the real living Stacey-May, back. Nothing! And I regret that. I do. But it was defensive, it wasn't murder.

The Hulk turned on everyone after Stacey-May the Head of the Project went down. He opened up at anyone and anything, except me.

I saw Counsellor Ciaran go down, shot in the back.

I heard the Hulk yelling at me, pointing the S & W at Seamus. "Come on, Coyote! That Taig Seamus is all yours."

I stepped up . . .

You'd have thought it would have been easy. I had motive coming out of my ears, centuries of Prod-love/Taig-hate, and I personally wanted to kill Seamus because of love. And, I had already tortured people. And, I had just killed somebody. And, I was the Alien, the Lizard. And, I had been named the Coyote, wildest and most lonesome of American mammals, on top of that. And Alco and the old pros said it was easier after you'd done the business, the coup de grace. But my first victim had not been intentional?

"Don't, please!" Seamus said.

So there I was, stuck, while Derry was running amok,

shooting and lobbing Molotov cocktails at the mansion; there
I was standing like a statue over Seamus with the house on fire
behind me, and I couldn't seem to pull that trigger. I mean,
Teresa and him were huddled together right in front of me
trying to cling to whatever they thought were their lives . . .

I heard police sirens in the distance. For a second—a fated
instant in time and space—I wanted to spare them. But then
Seamus squealed like a stuck pig: "For the love of God, no!"

For the love of God. For the love of God! That made me
remember I had always hated Seamus because my fore-
father-figures had always hated his fore-father-figures. I'd
always intended to kill Seamus, but not because of the way
Teresa was holding him and he her; because he was my
enemy, he was what made me "me"; he was what love, the
love of the Father and His group, His religion, His society,
His violence would and should be visited on.

I know now, way too late, that I was in error, and it was
the error of Terror. I was not the wrath of God. Seamus was
not my real enemy. Seamus was a son himself, a victim of
his Taigy emanation of the Father. What I'd done, what I'd
done was, rather than kill Da, rather than murder the primal Father himself . . .

I killed the son.

Bang! One shot through the heart. And with a banshee
wail from Teresa, Seamus was gone.

And for what? All for love.

If I could, I'd take it back. I'd journey back in time and

space like a shaman to magic him back to life, but I'm not a real shaman. Magic doesn't exist. I can't bring Seamus, my first son-sacrifice, Seamus my unknown hero, back from the dead. I have barely enough power to raise my self from there, the Void, this second time, to relive this part of my life for you prodigal sons out there. Barely enough power to project away from the negation of prison life.

The absence of friends. The missing of family. No job. No money. No meaning. Nothing normal. This is all I have had for fifteen years now. All I will have forever. Perhaps you prodigals can understand that I have to take it, but that this is more of a blessed curse than I deserve?

The Hulk, while roaring "The Sash," had killed and injured upward of fifteen Projectees by the time I'd taken to kill Seamus.

Eight Taigs.

The rest, Prods.

Among the as yet unnamed dead were Merrick Stulz and that wee fucker Joe Shanahan. I didn't mind so terribly that they bought it, but the others—wee Sorcha from the jumbo jet, Kelly the mother-virgin, and quiet Counsellor Kate, well, I regret that.

Yeah, I do.

Among the list of injured was Big Michael, who'd been shot through the right arm.

Everyone who wasn't dead or injured, like Helmut and

Phil, had legged it to the trees or swum out into the lake or done whatever it took to survive. With no more targets to blast with his hand-cannon, and somehow having lost his balaclava, the Hulk returned from his happy hunting.

The fact that sirens were wailing, calling to us, the cops finally responding to Tiara's call; getting nearer, the advance SWAT units powering up the far side of Lakeshore Drive, did not seem to faze him at all.

"Wow! Did you see that?" he said. "The way that bitch Kelly's head just blew apart."

"Nah," I said.

The Hulk looked down at Seamus. "Nice one, Coyote. You did it. Now do her too!"

I stepped up over the wailing Teresa. I pointed the Beretta at her heart.

"Do her!" he told me.

"Nah."

"Do it!"

"Nah, I can't."

"I'll do her for you then!" he said and pushed me out of the way.

Now, you know the way love made me a Judas once before? Well, it was to do so again. Right there. Right then. Rearing its ugly head, all unexpected like. See I looked at Teresa's closed crying eyes and I couldn't bear to see her hurt. Even after everything. I couldn't allow Derry to do it. I leveled the Beretta at his head and told him, "Leave her alone."

The Hulk looked into the barrel of the gun, then at me, the Alien in me. His eyes glowing green radioactive surprise but I could see he wasn't going to stop.

"That's enough!" I told him. "Don't do it!"

But the Hulk in his rage never stops. He'll pick you up and throw you through the air and you'll land in the barbecue and be covered in sausages while you burn alive . . .

That is, unless you shoot him right between the eyes at point-blank range. Like I did with Derry.

Yeah, I know, I know, what about my Loyalist loyalty, brotherhood unto death? I know, it was like criminal Cain in the name of the Father slaying Abel, like the first brotherly love-killing all over again.

I can't tell you how much I miss Derry.

Like crazy? Though that sounds like the way a homo'd put it. Like hell? Vacuous, but too shallow, too American. Like the Void? Almost works if you really and unreally understand what that is. But I can't really come up with anything that original, or individual. See nothing sums up nothing; loss, group-inflicted loss, like that. Words fail to deal with nothing, with death, killing, the negation of life.

And Teresa. Aw, I miss her too.

I saved her life, you know, like?

I took Derry's, and gave mine to save hers.

But wouldn't you know, like a wild skinhead deer, Teresa ran a mile from me when she saw the SWAT cars skid to a wailing halt outside the house. Who can blame her? Not me, not really.

I called after her. But she kept running.

I tore off my balaclava. I dropped the Beretta. I let Big Michael grab it and hold it on me as I stood there in the smoke and carnage and watched Teresa the Taig deer go. It was actually a beautiful sight what with the blue of the lake and everything behind her. The sort of tragic melodramatic romantic shot you should end a Hollywood movie on. Because it's life-affirming. Because it's love-affirming. Because it's hero-affirming. Because it's group-affirming. Because it's father-affirming. Because it's God-affirming.

This isn't a movie though. It's just my story. And I personally would blow chunks if it ended like that. Yeah, and there's things to be said about the failure of Project Ulster, and whether the peace process back home will ever bring peace, and whether or not the Americans will ever introduce gun controls. These are the sort of things that should be said at the end of a book like this, aren't they?

But, you know what? Nothing. I'll leave it there. Yeah. That's all I'm going to say. I could probably tell you loads more in some rambling epilogue about how the SS SWAT came and arrested me brutally and how claustrophobic it felt that first night in the cell, and how it felt before and during and after the trial to hear the Project, America, Ulster, even my own Ma and Da condemn me as "a fourteen-year-old monster." But I won't, because it means nothing to an individual like me now. I could bang on about how I became a UFF folk hero back home and how in 1994 Alco and the CLMC (Combined Loyalist Military Command) fought to have me deported to serve the rest of my time in the Maze. But I don't want to because it means nothing to an individual like me and I refused their offer point-blank. And yeah, if I wanted, I could finish up by telling you the ongoing story about the death threats from both the Northern Irish and American families of the dead which have confined me to an Isolation cell for most of my sentence. But all-told what does another miscarriage of patriarchal justice matter? The story improper, it's over.